Father War

FATHER
WAR

—

THOMAS DOHERTY

Matador
9 Priory Business Park,
Wistow Road, Kibworth Beauchamp,
Leicestershire. LE8 0RX
Tel: 0116 279 2299
Email: books@troubador.co.uk
Web: www.troubador.co.uk/matador
Twitter: @matadorbooks

ISBN 978 1 800 46272 4

British Library Cataloguing in Publication Data.
A catalogue record for this book is available from the British Library.

Printed and bound in Great Britain by 4edge Limited
Typeset in 12pt Adobe Jenson Pro by Troubador Publishing Ltd, Leicester, UK

Matador is an imprint of Troubador Publishing Ltd

In memory of David and Marion Stocking

Well travelled, well read, well informed,
he was a stranger in the world.
Evelyn Waugh
Unconditional Surrender

1945

———

THE LETTERS HIS MOTHER RUSHED TO THE MAILBOX for came from 'Jack'. Then one day she crumpled a letter and ran from the kitchen crying, "What are we going to do?" That was the end of 'Jack'. Now at mealtimes she grumbled about 'that stinker... that heel... that cheat'.

That's all young John Spenser knew as he tagged along behind his mother through one coach after another. The train was packed with men in khaki. They slumped and sprawled – a gaping mouth here, dribbles of sick down a shirtfront there, rangy legs to trip over all along the aisle – oblivious to the little boy who worshipped soldiers. John couldn't believe these were the same GIs praised on the news every night, the ones who took prisoners by the mile, rescued the suffering, and made foul places clean again.

They'd been celebrating, she told him in a whisper. Their war was over, their waiting was over, and soon they would disappear into everyday life like ordinary people.

But his mother's waiting wasn't over. 'That stinker' was back from the war, and she had 'business' to settle with him.

Row after row of lookalike buildings drifted by the window as the train slowed. The soldiers came alive, yawning and grouching. Soon they jammed the aisle. His mother waited until they flooded onto the platform before taking John's hand and leading him down the steps into fresh air and sunlight, then after a short walk into a smoky room filled with soldiers and families.

The tables were full so she helped him onto a stool at the lunch counter. He froze. He couldn't believe what he was seeing. The man working the grill wore a shirt with the letters PW stamped on the back. He was John's first live German and he was doing the work of teenaged girls. No one came up to settle old scores or even paid attention. When the man slid a grilled cheese sandwich under his nose, John was certain he had seen those hands before in a newsreel – opening a furnace door.

All around, soldiers laughed and blew smoke at the ceiling even as the Devil himself stabbed their sandwiches with a toothpick.

Out of the haze, a figure swooped over him, smothering him in a bear hug and hefting him high overhead. He heard his mother say, "Oh no, you don't!" Before John could catch his breath he was back on his stool, alone, and the two grown-ups were off huddling together. Someone had to keep an eye on the German, so that's what he did until his mother was back beside him, digging through her purse for something she couldn't find. The hugging soldier was gone.

After dark she pulled him along a wooden sidewalk past one boxy barracks after another, across a muddy street and through a doorway into lights and music and perfume and cigarette smoke where soldiers and women danced to songs his mother listened to on the radio. She dragged him up a circling staircase, and at the very top they stood by a guardrail looking down on the gliding figures.

Two of those figures drifted away from the dancers and looked up at his mother, the hugging soldier from the lunch counter and a woman much brighter than his mother, fancier. They held hands. Like his mother, John stared at them, pressing his face between spindles under the guardrail. She was pretty, and unlike his mother she didn't seem to be mad about anything.

Later she made him crawl under an army blanket in a room of raw wood walls. She told him to go to sleep, but he kept watching her. The last thing he remembered was his mother sitting on her bed, ignoring the magazine in her lap and staring at the door whenever footsteps went by in the hall. If this was what our lives would be like from now on, he thought, then give me black-outs, brooding, a hunger for letters. Give me voices crackling from across the sea. Give me newsreels. Give me war.

1989

―――――

THERE IT WAS AGAIN – HONORA'S ELBOW.

Oh how Jack Hagan loved his naps, especially after two vodka miniatures thirty thousand feet over the Pacific. He roused himself back into a tight little world of knees and nodding heads. Duty called.

"Sorry, darling," she said, the words gurgling through the goop in her airway. "I can't wait."

Honora clung to Jack's arm as they lumbered up the aisle. Once again sullen faces turned to take in their slow-motion potty run. To non-sleepers bored out of their wits they had become the only show in town.

"You know what they're thinking, don't you?" he muttered. "They think we're trying to join the Mile High Club."

"Ha!" she croaked. She gave his arm a feeble squeeze. "You filthy old dog."

"What about vile?" he said. "Don't I make the grade anymore?"

Oh, how she struggled to breathe. "As vile as ever,

dearie," she assured him. "Vile, filthy, disgusting – whatever you like. Just drag me to a little room where I can collapse and breathe. I'm suffocating in this crowd."

He patted her cold hand. "Hang in there, kiddo."

If only she'd eat something, but just the sight of food made her queasy. There had been a burst of bright-eyed eagerness when they climbed aboard at Melbourne, but by Sydney she was pale and withdrawn – traveler's gloom, he assumed – and things had only gotten worse since.

Glancing over the onlookers Jack thought, you should be so lucky. Honora was no longer the fresh young beauty Douglas MacArthur's colonels had lusted after fifty years ago when she delivered flowers to the Menzies Hotel every morning, not by a long shot, but she was still his prize of a lifetime, his wisecracking beauty, and the source of everything good in his life.

Back then Jack had been a rifleman in a green infantry division just off the boat after weeks at sea. Melbourne was a stop on the way to the beaches of Queensland to confront the all-but-certain Japanese invasion. But for Jack Hagan, Melbourne changed everything. In high school he'd boasted to his pals that he was going to sign up for typing. They were killing time in the lunch room, and he had his eye on a girl at another table. His buddies insisted he didn't have the guts, but by the end of the semester he was averaging thirty-five words a minute, the only boy in class. His pay off was the girl. As a couple they were a big deal for a few years, the blue-collar kid and the pretty girl from the big house on a hill.

But in Melbourne that class paid off again in a most unexpected way. It may even have saved his life. His days as a rifleman ended. He was assigned to a typing pool housed in the gym of a girls' high school. His new bosses were colonels and majors – low-level members of MacArthur's so-called 'Bataan Gang'. Damned as cowards by the fighting men they'd left behind on Bataan and Corregidor, they had been greeted as heroes by desperate Aussies.

Liberated from the cattle-call life of troop ships and tent cities, Hagan found himself living like a civilian in uniform – big city streets full of admiring passers-by, hot meals, a real bed with clean sheets, and morning courier duty to and from the Menzies, where he had first laid eyes on that spectacular flower girl. The rest of the day he pecked away at a Remington office model. In lovely Melbourne Jack Hagan became a new man.

His old outfit had barely gotten used to life in their new tent city near Brisbane before they were set in motion again, this time into a steamy, godforsaken corner of Papua New Guinea. According to an officer who was at the airstrip when, months later, the fever-wracked survivors were ferried back to Brisbane, they looked like Jesus on the cross. Meanwhile in Melbourne Hagan had become seriously involved with the flower girl.

"Uh oh," Jack said. "Trouble ahead." On their last trip up the aisle all the bathrooms had been occupied, but at least the wait had been short. This time there was a line. He counted four heads plus a little girl with her mother, maybe more out of sight behind the curtain. "Looks like a long wait."

"Jack, I *hate* this!" she wheezed. "Do something!" Sweat beaded around her ashen lips.

He took a deep breath: "Okay. Hold on."

"Coming through," he announced, pressing against the woman in front of him. Heads turned, none of them friendly. "Awfully sorry, but we've got to get through. Thank you... Oops, sorry..." He shuffled Honora past resisting bodies that gave way only after her face came into view. "I know, I know. I'd be bummed too. We're jumping the queue, but only because we're desperate."

Emerging at the head of the line, he went knocking on doors. "Very urgent need here! Please hurry! Very urgent need here...!" Two doors opposite one another came open at the same time. He blocked the aisle, waiting for those bodies to vacate, then poked his head into the room on the left. He came out wincing. "Monkey house!" he whispered into her ear. To the right a woman was trying to slide past him to the other vacancy, but he blocked her with his arm, and with Honora nearly tripping over his leaning body he gave that room a sniff. "Bacon!" he announced. "Like breakfast at home. This one's for you."

Her knees were unreliable, she mumbled to herself, and she could barely stay upright without support, and so as she braced herself against the sink in a trembling plastic closet high above the ocean, he took over. It was nearly impossible for him to get a grip on those jellyfish-slick synthetics, but eventually he managed to scoot everything down to her puffy ankles, then helped her to pivot and sit with a gasp. "Doing okay?" he asked. She nodded her weary head. Poor Honora. His quick-witted, bright-eyed beauty of long ago had turned inward, awkward, and frail.

He stepped outside, closed the door and leaned his back against it, standing guard. People he had bulldozed aside looked on. He could almost feel their hostility. "Damn shame how they cram us in these days. And I thought a troop ship was bad. I'd love to buy you all a drink, but that would only make things worse, wouldn't it?" To the little girl he said, "I hope you're next, sweetie. I know what it's like to wait."

His temporary assignment lasted to the end of the war. Just as he was preparing to ship home, Honora told him she was pregnant. She begged him to hurry back after discharge and join the family business, but he urged her to join him in America instead. She gave in and spent the next two years in a university trailer park outside of Madison where every day she fought her way through a blizzard of drying nappies to the mailbox, praying for a letter from Mum. Hagan preferred male companionship in State Street dives to the silent agony of the library. His one attempt to mend fences from that previous relationship cost him a night in jail. His homecoming had turned into a fiasco for him and a marathon of loneliness for Honora. It was confirmation of what they'd each secretly suspected all along. He was not college material. It was Honora's turn to decide what next. For her it would be a homecoming; for him, a career in the flower business in a city he hadn't even heard of until the army deposited him there. So here they were at the other end of a life of sun, smoke, gin and mostly easy living, and what a life it had been. They knew from the example of Honora's parents how it would turn out. Even the good life took a toll.

But in a foreign city that became more of a home to him than home had ever been, he was transformed into a privileged fella with a delectable girl and a job that required little more than a good heart, a gift of gab, and a high capacity for drink. Flowers, of all damn things! Honora's relatives operated the greenhouses and trucked the goods into the city. His job was to sell them. He serviced accounts: funeral homes, houses of worship, hotels. For years Honora had been the bright face of the business to major customers, but after Jack learned the trade she was thrilled to stay home with the account books and the babies. In some ways he was better suited to being the face of the business anyway. Honora hated golf and soon wearied of polite conversation whereas he loved afternoons under the sun and could buddy up with just about anyone. She was the dazzling lure that had hooked the customers. He was the companionable guy who kept them coming back.

From time to time as he waited, his right hand drifted to his empty shirt pocket. Except for the fact that his next smoke was at least a dozen hours away, he had no complaints. He often thought back to the eve of his tenth birthday when it had first occurred to him that he would never see single digits again. Life seemed a relentless one-way trip, and at the end you'd feel gypped. Instead, here he was many decades later, barrel-chested, short of breath and hopelessly constipated, his face and scalp nicked with scars where cancers had been cut out, phlegm-throated and liver-spotted, dutifully marking time until his old gal did her business, and yet he was blissfully free of grievances of any kind, the beneficiary of a good life he'd done nothing to deserve. Better men had suffered longer and died sooner. On weekends at Portsea they'd trudge up from the beach hand in hand, giddy from sun and gin, and she'd glance at his gaping mouth and murmur, "Scooping krill again, dearie?"

This would be their final visit. He wouldn't have bothered but for a name that appeared in *The Stalker*, his old outfit's newsletter. The Bold Eagle veterans' club was turning Fort Palmer's old Building One into a museum and had hired a guy name John Spenser to run it. What a shock seeing that name associated with *his* veterans' club. Hagan had a son named John Spenser, though he didn't know him and had met him only briefly eons ago. The issue had remained an open wound ever since. Probably there were many John Spensers in the world, but it seemed more than coincidental that one of them would end up at Fort Palmer. The news rattled him and got him thinking.

Fortunately Honora had loose ends of her own to settle or she'd never have agreed to come along. Her latest onset of bronchitis had put them three weeks behind schedule. They had already missed the reunion and with it a chance to meet up with any of the fellas, but his primary mission was unchanged. After previous reunions they'd headed to the Mall of America and toured the shore of Lake Superior. One year they spent a week at a resort in Door Peninsula run by a fellow Bold Eagle vet. They had visited New York, Chicago, and Washington DC. But this trip would be stripped down to essentials. Over and back. A final goodbye to the USA.

Never before had it seemed such an ordeal. Twenty-four hours plus from Melbourne to Sidney to Honolulu to San Francisco to Chicago, then half a day in a rental car. Well, so what? Old people were climbing Mount Everest these days. If he could put to rest the business that had been on his mind forever, a little mortification along the way would be a small price to pay.

For a second time the stewardess stood in the aisle peering at him. She looked concerned. "Everything okay?" she said.

He checked his watch, then tapped on the door. "Hey kiddo, what's up? Fall asleep?"

1958

———

JOHN SPENSER KNEW WHEN HE FIRST SAW HER THAT he should keep his mouth shut. Nothing good could come of it. He had learned early in life how these things turned out. There would be trouble – certainly for him and probably for her too. It would be a minefield, but the urge to take that first step was becoming irresistible. Sometimes people did stupid things because they just couldn't help it. In idle moments his mother had assured him that she was all for courtship and happily ever after, but that's not how her life had turned out. Not by a long shot.

Still, there she was again, the new girl, white Keds, bandana skirt, pink cardigan and books cradled in her arms. Like the others she was leaning against the wall of the Edison Building on the other side of the asphalt basketball court, soaking up the sun and chattering with the girls, waiting for the morning bell. Spenser watched from the third-floor study hall in Old Main with a half dozen other senior boys. If he didn't make a move, it was only a matter of time before someone else did.

He kept reminding himself that in six months he would start a new life at the university and she would be history. But would she? Could he live the rest of his life knowing that to her he didn't exist?

Then one morning he opened his damn mouth. "So who is she?"

His mother used to stand at the sink punishing insubordinate utensils. "Damn you!" she'd hiss. "Damn you." She lost arguments with a folding lawn chair: "Damn you!" Things had not worked out.

Once she showed him a snapshot from long ago of his father in uniform. They were arm in arm, two happy people in love. That was before his father was sent overseas and dropped out of her life. He died 'somewhere in Germany.' His mission had been so secret that that's all she'd ever been able to learn.

They lived with a sense of unfinished business. Years passed. He looked for answers in his grandparents' magazines. 'Embattled Peking... Paris: Thunder from the Left...' Women wept over the passing coffin of a leader bullied to death by Russians. 'Terror in the Holy Land... The front in Greece is everywhere...' Observers saw ominous signs in the transfer of certain ports from one power to another, in the failure of conference after conference. Always a sense of things spinning out of control.

His path was set. Your country is a risk. Pay attention. Don't get distracted. You have a job to do.

Korea was next, and years later on the evening news he watched the comings and goings at an airbase near Saigon, our guy in a white suit bounding down the ramp to connect with their guy in starched fatigues and dark glasses waiting below. A flashbulb glare of post-explosion carnage in a movie theater. An ambulance speeding away from a bombed sidewalk cafe. Experts carried on about the monks and students, the Hoa Hoa, the Boa Dai, the Binh Xuyen, the Chinese tycoons of Cholon, the gangsters of Macao and forces said to be gathering in the misty highlands...

But no one understood, not our guy with his hand outstretched and certainly not theirs, placidly offering his own. Wise old voices issued warnings, but it was too late. In Asia, in Europe, in places unknown, frontiers were being infiltrated. A man could be converted before your eyes and you wouldn't even notice. That stain on the newsreel globe was spreading. We had to go in.

The girl's name was Deidre Conlin, and the day after Spenser asked the fatal question she locked eyeballs with him in the hall between classes. A faint scent of clove lingered. Never before had he ventured alone into the hangout called The Loft, but that Friday night he stepped into the light and the music, and in no time Deidre Conlin was in his face. "Want to learn to slow dance?" she said.

Friday nights became dancing nights, the warmth of her, the dizzying scent of clove and something beyond it, beyond soap and armpit cream – vapors from her real self. There were moments when he turned clingy and misty-headed.

"Think about all those poor girls," his mother said as year after year he had passed up the homecoming dance and then the spring dance. She couldn't imagine anyone leaving high school without memories of at least one big dance. His last chance was coming up soon. The theme of the spring dance this year was 'Finale'. Surely he wasn't going to miss out on this one too, was he?

It was a trap of his own making. Now two women were watching him and counting down the days. One Saturday morning he approached the dreaded telephone knowing that he would hate himself no matter what.

He expected Deidre to be nervous too, but she was more than nervous. Desperate. "I almost asked you what took so long," she said. "Oops! Forget I said that." Did he even have a car? She thought her dad would loan him theirs. "You have a license, don't you?"

A few days before the dance his mother took him out for supper. There were things she wanted him to know – protocol: meeting the parents, dealing with the corsage and so on, just little stuff to get the evening off to a smooth start. He wasn't crazy about these occasional outings. He didn't know other guys who went to restaurants with their mothers. During all those years of Friday night fish fries and weeknight specials in canopied roadhouses there never was a meal that seemed to go right. Why this table, suspiciously removed from the well-dressed crowd, in an archipelago unto themselves? Or this one, where the Everly Brothers on the jukebox threatened to explode the vinegar cruet? At intervals the kitchen door flew open and filled the silence above their struggling candle with a view of boiler-room faces caught off guard. Sometimes it was nothing more than a hovering dissonance that she detected, mischief in the metaphysics of this particular spot that called for discreet adjustments right away. For years she wove these complicated patterns from table to unsatisfactory table, never quite finding the one God had intended just for them.

This time it was the waitress. She wouldn't look away from the pad in her hand and ignored his mother's pleasantries. *Rude* was the word she used. Dining out was supposed to be a pleasant experience. She decided that the manager should be told about this girl. John shook his head. Not me. Her jaw was set. "I want another waitress."

"They're rushed, Mom. It's a busy night."

"People can still smile and look at you. If you were the manager wouldn't you want to know about her?"

He shut up and went deaf. Sometimes that was all you could do.

Saturday morning John picked up the corsage and retrieved his suit from the cleaners. Back home he tried to break in new shoes while steeling himself for obstacles ahead. His wet, wimpy hand would confirm her father's every suspicion about him, and God forbid anything happened to his granddad's new Buick. Hanging over everything was Deidre's mysterious life. His mother used to go on about women whose husbands were away at war and how they spent their days doing all the right things, looking after the kids and so on, but at night they went out hunting for sailors. You just never knew.

He submitted to his mother's inspection. His grandmother looked on, beaming and muttering flattery, trying to boost his courage. As he eased the Buick out of the garage, she came out of the back porch waving the box containing Deidre's corsage.

He headed into the countryside. By now folks who had

spent the day in town were home, but it was too early for the night-time prowlers and party seekers so he had the road to himself. He pulled over beside a corn field, undid his tie and dropped the corsage out the passenger window. He continued north past the gravel pit and nursery fields lined with saplings into the shadowy woods of the Bitterman Hills. The intersection in the village of New Cardiff was lit by a single street light. The pay phone on the corner seemed almost to beckon to him, but he knew that no excuse he could come up with now would make a difference.

The country school turned roadhouse was lit up and surrounded by cars. The glow over the back lot would be a soft ball game. He parked and sat for a minute with the door open, listening to voices from the field. He laid his suit coat across the back seat. Even without his jacket and tie he was overdressed in this crowd. He headed for the bleachers. Women and kids filled the bottom rows, but the top two were empty. With an evening to kill he'd need room to stretch out in comfort, if comfort was possible under the circumstances.

What he was doing went beyond mere cowardice. He'd lost his way. That could not happen again. No more distractions, no baggage, not even the likes of Deidre Conlin. That's what he kept telling himself while killing time up there under the lights.

1 9 8 9

———

J ACK HAGAN WAS SHAKING WHEN HE CALLED THE
girls from San Francisco. He dreaded what he had to
tell them, but they took the news well. It occurred to him
that they were better prepared than he was. Mostly they
seemed concerned about him. How was he taking it? Was
there anything they could do? He breathed easier then.
He was relieved, flattered even. He promised that he'd
bring their mother home. She'd get the grand send-off she
deserved and end up next to her parents where, in time,
he would join her.

Three days later he drove north from O'Hare worried
about what lay ahead. Living half a world away from the
old gang, he tended to forget that in the most crucial,
life-altering way he stood apart from other Bold Eagle
veterans. Only on the eve of a reunion did that fact settle
over him like a bad odor. They went into the jungle and he
had not. Until the day of his separation from the division
he had been as likely as any to die of a raging infection, to
get lost on patrol and end up gutted with his balls stuffed

in his mouth, to be machine-gunned in a bungled night attack, or to be damned as a coward by some sneering lackey of MacArthur's. Instead he'd spent the war in comfort, wearing clean underwear and sitting at a desk or behind the wheel of a sedan. There was nothing he could have done to change any of that.

At his first reunion he showed up in a T-shirt that said, MY REMINGTON WAS A TYPEWRITER. Some of the guys from the Drumlin company, the ones he'd gone through high school with and played ball with, seemed to get a kick out of it, so the next time he had one made up that read:

> LEFT BEHIND BECAUSE –
> Sick with a fever?   No!
> Locked in the stockade?   No!
> Typed like a demon?   YES!

Once again some of the Drumlin gang caught on, but others had trouble remembering him. Some even seemed reluctant to shake his hand. He wasn't exactly an outcast, but he sometimes felt like one. Was it worth thousands of dollars and all the hassles of intercontinental travel only to end up feeling like he didn't belong?

Such were the thoughts he confessed to Honora on the long drive north. It seemed so natural, so *inevitable* to open up to her now. On the approach to earlier reunions he'd been wretched with uncertainty. Honora had kept her mouth shut. She knew better than to pry. This time he felt free to speak his mind. Bitchy little doubts and grievances about this so-called buddy and that ignorant lieutenant that he'd been stashing away for decades he spread before her like fragments from an archaeological dig, certain of her sympathy and understanding. It was liberating.

On the seat beside him was a container about the size of a small music box, a white lid on a black base. The funeral home people had assured him it was both practical and sturdy and thus a good choice for a traveling man. As a bonus it was also biodegradable. He felt chintzy about the price, but ceramic was fragile and brass was heavy. Honora would have understood.

So for once he would arrive at Old Camp Palmer dread-free. The reunion was over, and it was only a name that drew him halfway across the world this time, not a lingering sense of camaraderie. He reminded himself that there was more than one John Spenser in the world. If the one running the museum was not his son, at least his conscience would be clear. He would have traveled the world to do the right thing, however belatedly. What more could be expected of him this late in life?

At least he wasn't on a tight schedule anymore. There was no need to rush home. Even as old habits kept him heading towards Camp Palmer, other options came to mind. After all, this was where he was born. He was back among old, familiar place names. Beloit was just ahead, then Janesville, and a half hour further along, Madison, State Street, Bascom Hill. And off to the west, Drumlin and old Drumlin High. A lot of unfinished business hereabouts came to mind, not just a guy with a familiar name.

* * *

At summer camp in the old days they'd been sent up these hills on cavalry patrol only to meet infantry troops coming downhill, also on patrol, the horses setting off little rock slides as each side bitched at the other, exchanging insults about the other guy's form of locomotion and the blisters it produced. Now he supposed he was driving up one of those same trails, though it had since been straightened and paved and was shaded over by row after row of pine trees planted long ago by the CCC.

Honora's snapshots of a guy named Dion DeLuca were in his shirt pocket with his smokes. She had taken a long time to confide in him. DeLuca had been a musician in the Bold Eagle division band, a clarinet player who also stepped up to the microphone to work his finger-popping Sinatra routine. Lecherous old colonels were not the only guys who had zeroed in on Honora, and DeLuca was the one she'd fallen for. Like so many Aussies she had been smitten by all things American, and what could have been more seductive, more *American*, than a dago crooner in khaki? In one of the photos she was cheek to cheek with the guy, and in the other he was pitching hot love at the microphone, while the women at his feet either swooned or cringed. It was hard to tell.

Okay, Hagan mused. No hard feelings. Honora had pulled herself together for this trip because she wanted answers. Though she was beyond caring at this point, Hagan was curious enough and loyal enough to her memory to pursue the issue with young Spenser anyway. If anyone had access to a database it would be the guy running the museum.

Shadows fell away and the car emerged into blue sky. The top of the bluff had undergone a CCC workover. It had been leveled, paved, and walled off from the ledge.

He parked, hefted the container from the seat, and approached the stone wall. The view was magnificent, as always. Below stretched the grassy plain where they had camped and marched and played ball, where smoke had drifted from the rifle range under Target Bluff. Still standing on the side of the hill across the plain but barely visible in the shade of protective oaks was the old headquarters building. Officially known as Building One, unofficially as The Lodge, it was a log edifice with a wide-brim roof and wrap-around porch, a ringer for the one John Wayne used to sashay out of swatting his leg with cavalry gloves and sniffing the air for Apaches. It overlooked a row of one-story brick barracks on the field below built by CCC workers during the Depression. The Lodge had been many things through the decades – state headquarters and armory, WPA barracks, stockade, and finally, officers' club for the Air Guard. In recent decades it had sat idle, an empty shell, only coming back to life during Bold Eagle reunions. As an almost sacred relic it was a natural choice for the museum, a shelter for whatever bits and pieces of a fading story that could still be pieced together from a distracted world already sick to death of such stories.

The sun was high, the air still, and peace reigned as he gently set the container on the top of the wall. This was a first for him, and he hesitated, uncertain how to proceed. He tentatively pried the lid and was amazed how little effort it took. It was like opening a box of chocolates. There she was, down in the shadows. "Just a big fuckin' joke, ain't it, m'dear?" he said in the silly brogue that typically emerged only when he was well into happy hour. "A big fuckin' joke, but a good one."

His fist came up leaking ribbons of ash. "Just a bit of you now, 'cause this is where it all started for me. There would have been no Australia and no Honora if not for Old Camp Palmer and a bunch of young pricks being made to feel like soldiers. Lots of nonsense here, but lots of fun too, prancing around in soldier clothes like big shots, marching and shooting and boozing. It all led me to you."

He bent into the wall and pitched the crumbles into space where the heavy bits fell away but the powdery stuff uncoiled like smoke and hung in the air shapeless and inert. He closed his eyes and raised his face to the sun. If there was a breeze he did not feel it. For the moment he was a grade schooler again, benumbed by the late summer blues, lazy, bored and lonesome, yet he wouldn't change a thing. He'd take the heat and stillness, even the world's indifference to little old him as long as it made no demands.

Hagan opened his eyes, expecting the smoke to be gone, but it still hovered just beyond reach. His eyes began to burn. Grit got caught in his throat. He sneezed. "Okay, m'dear. No more. The rest goes home. I promise."

Fever-faced and teary-eyed he drove back down to the interstate and continued a few miles north to the main gate. The guard house was empty, the gate open, and soon he was over the train tracks and through the tree line. Here the road diverged. A left turn would take him north to so-called New Camp Palmer, a vast, hilly training ground with its own sprawling city of grey barracks, mess halls and motor pools that had been thrown up in a rush like dozens of other camps across the country in the early forties. A right turn led to placid Old Camp Palmer where the threadbare Bold Eagle division of the twenties and thirties had kept alive old army rituals and a what-the-hell spirit out of sight of a civilian world turned sour on all things military by the horrors of the so-called war to end all wars.

It occurred to him that he was getting ahead of himself. An old hand at the art of putting strangers at ease, he wasn't so sure his magic would work on a son whose world he had never been part of. He had plenty of practice reading the other guy and keeping things loose, and he had some easy-does-it opening lines in mind. But with the encounter possibly just minutes away he was having second thoughts. With Honora at his side he would have been more confident. He dreaded a dustup. Things had to be under control, light and easy, no hard feelings, yet he had delayed for so long.

A rest area with a picnic table and public toilets came into view just in time. He parked and got out of the car. He had the place to himself. His hand went to his shirt pocket and plucked out a cigarette. A piss, a smoke, a few minutes in the shade to think things through. At times like this he sure missed her company, but what he felt was not exactly grief, or what he thought grief should be. It was more like a melancholy fondness at the loss of an old partner. There was something almost sweet about the feeling, like an old dance song coming out of the blue. Maybe grief would strike later. He had to admit that what gripped him now was more like excitement. It was dawning on him – a bit shamefully, he had to admit – that he was free. He was like a kid heading outside into sunshine and grassy smells after a long illness in a dark room, desperate to catch up with all he'd missed out on. He reminded himself that there was no rush, not anymore. He had all the time in the world. How was he holding up? Better than he would admit to his daughters.

A pair of army trucks, old deuce and a halfs, came slowly groaning along the dirt road from Old Camp and passed him by, apparently heading to New Camp. On the back of the first was a mishmash of bundles and cartons and file cabinets, but it was the stuff on the second truck that caught Jack's eye. A half dozen tall glass cases of the kind you might find in a museum had been draped in protective quilting and securely strapped to the bed of the truck along with racks of what appeared to be military clothing of various types.

Strange. If the museum was in old Building One in Old Camp, what was this stuff, and why was it heading out?

1967

———

Second Lieutenant John Spenser poked his head between the tent flaps into the wake-up smells of coffee and bacon. "Hey Sarge, where's the crapper?"

He'd slept through thunder and drum rolls of rain lashing his canvas roof, but when a storm erupted in his gut he came jolting upright, full of panic. It was 0430. He clawed open the mosquito net, pulled on his boots and web gear, grabbed his steel pot and fumbled outside into the same downpour that soaked enemy soldiers in the hills.

In the mess tent last night someone said the NVA had broken in on the artillery net boasting they were going to overrun the camp. Spenser hadn't gotten his bearings yet. He tried to read the faces around him. Mouths were stuffed, jaws churned, eyelids were at half mast. Didn't they care? Didn't they talk about these things?

The mess sergeant looked up from his mug and cigarette. His hat was the whitest thing Spenser had seen since his flight from California three weeks ago. "Down the trail. Follow your nose."

He crashed into the water trailer. No time to catch his breath. Further along, he was up to his ankles in mud. The mess sergeant was right. He was getting close. His waving hand caught a rope.

This was all new to him. He'd been assigned to army intelligence in Saigon. His job was to transport sealed pouches. He spent much of his time on helicopters. It suited his temperament. The Huey would land, he'd locate a headquarters tent or bunker, and before his ears popped and voices began to make sense he was off again. They had sent him up to the Highlands with a list of names and profiles. They told him it was a big deal. Key figures had disappeared from their usual haunts, possibly back into the field, possibly even way up here.

Inside he unharnessed his web gear, dumped the bundle into his upside down helmet on the floor, dropped his pants and sat with a gasp on the wooden seat. He moaned and whimpered sounds of gratitude and relief. He had not humiliated himself. Nothing else mattered. Let them drop in their mortar rounds. Let them come sneaking through the wire and wet grass.

He ran a hand over his face. Should he have shaved last night or would he have time this morning? Could he fill his steel pot from the water trailer or was that just for the cooks? He'd have to see how others handled it.

That's when he realized he was not alone. Pants were being pulled up and cinched. Had he ruined a private moment?

A sling rattled against a rifle stock and a tent flap flew open on the opposite end, facing the hills. "Have a good one," Spenser said, expecting to hear boots on duckboard. But the figure glided away without a sound. Was he barefooted? Or – could it be? – was he wearing sandals made from old tires?

Everywhere, this sense of a storm about to break. On an island crowned with huge orange antennas, a security sergeant led him up into a guard tower chilled by breezes off the South China Sea. From the tower at twilight, Nha Trang and Cam Ranh might have been glitzy resort towns so festive was the glow they sent rippling across the bay. Guys extended their enlistments to stay at a place like this. A solitary shift in an air-conditioned hut monitoring banks of radio relay equipment, then horseshoes, volleyball, an evening swim and a movie under the stars. It was the kind of duty they didn't want anyone else to know about.

But even with his machine guns and grenade launchers and concertina wire laced with trip flares, the sergeant had grown leery of the fishing boats below and of whatever might emerge from the dark mainland to the north. Even here the good life was turning sour.

Along the coast at Vung Tau, an MP lieutenant was worn down from a succession of night alerts which always petered out at first light into a headachy suspicion that he had left some essential task undone. In the red dust of Long Binh the engineers rushed to assemble a prefabricated city in which to gather the many support outfits scattered around Saigon. Tanks roamed the perimeter. Airborne battalions hopscotched throughout the area to keep the enemy off balance. Helicopters patrolled the road to Saigon.

Sometimes at night Spenser woke chilled by the ceiling fan. Running a hand over his ribs, he considered how easy it would be for them to penetrate the tropical openness of this suburban billet. Silently over the wall, a flimsy lock to pick or screen to remove. They could be lurking in the hallways right now, mapping the place for their big day.

But in the dawn light he felt remarkably level-headed. A scheme of things was falling into place. No one asked his opinion when they sent him off cuffed to a briefcase full of envelopes stamped with big red warnings, but he had a sense of what the lifers upstairs were brooding about. Summaries of prisoner interrogations, reports from the Vietnamese police, and other odds and ends passed over his desk. He read them all, whether intended for his eyes or not.

Some guys let the garbage and ingratitude sour them on the Vietnamese but not Spenser. While the others confined their explorations to the bars and steam baths or joined the mob at the big PX, he hired a cyclo and got to know the city. At the controls behind him, a scrawny, cat-whiskered mercenary in dark glasses on a sputtering wreck of a motorcycle. Ahead, all of Saigon.

On the grassy bank of the Saigon River, Chinamen in pajamas appeared to go through a slow-motion simulation of calisthenics while on a warship behind them ranks of Korean sailors bellowed and stomped through the real thing. At the central market baskets of squawking animals were passed from battered Dodge buses to gaggles of waiting peasants. A woman went by in a pedicab with a pig sprawled across her lap. They sped through a shady grid of washed and perfumed European boulevards and gilded facades which gave way to courtyards dense with hanging laundry and yammering women, then to narrow streets where his eyes burned from the reek of urine, charcoal smoke and fermenting waste, emerging finally into neighborhoods of frail structures and swallow-boned people in black. Bright pools of produce and utensils spilled onto the walks from open-front shops. Nets of gun-blue flies hovered over puddles in the unpaved streets. Children ran alongside the cyclo, hands extended: "You! You! You...!"

Some nights he stayed up until dawn with his new Japanese radio, searching for news and trying to make sense of the random bits of data he'd come across: "BBC Southeast Asia now ceases transmission on this frequency. The East African transmission continues..." "They said Nazareth was a lousy town, a looked-down-upon dirty town. They said nothing good would ever come out of that town..." In the weary cadence of a cab dispatcher, an air controller warned pilots of small arms fire along the Mekong. Between stations came an awesome static like the roar of a distant mob.

One day on a routine run to army headquarters at Tan Son Nhut airbase John broke with tradition and directed Mr Dinh out the back door, so to speak, through subdivisions of mint-green barracks and a futuristic radar complex into a wasteland marked by relics of an earlier war, abandoned guard towers and the skeletons of junked airplanes. Along the dirt road women hawked lukewarm bottles of Coke and beer to soldiers rumbling through on garbage runs. Further along, scavengers waded through smoldering mounds, mining for odd bits of metal, discarded footwear and packing cartons.

Just beyond the pall of smoke a grassy rise stood over the debris like a castaway's island. An upended World War Two fighter plane was its palm tree. The Vietnamese Special Police reported that this poisoned no man's land had become home to a group of street kids. Beggars, peddlers and shoeshine hustlers, they had migrated from the riverfront. What were they doing way out here, far from their clientele on Tudo and Cong Ly streets?

Spenser's panel truck emerged onto Plantation Road and a boomtown crossroads where men lounged in dim cafes under a profusion of calendars, gazing into the traffic, which at this hour was mostly army green with a sprinkling of blue and yellow taxis, his old VC regular possibly among them. Spenser had spotted him first at the central market where contraband from the countryside arrived every morning with peasants and their produce. The Vietnamese police had intercepted a letter from his wife. Did he exercise in the early morning while the air was still fresh? Did he avoid the Chinese cafes in Cholon where government spies hung out and the food was unclean? His cover as taxi driver provided easy access to the airbase and its environs, possibly including that wasteland where the street toughs had recently taken up residence.

Spenser got out of the truck and sent Mr Dinh back to the motor pool. On foot, he backtracked past graves of French nuns and a crumbling sandbag bunker that had once stood guard over the field. Inside the map case over his shoulder were binoculars and his ancient service automatic with two full magazines.

Twenty minutes later he was kneeling in a rusted, urine-scented guard tower, swatting mosquitoes and gazing through the binoculars. This was not like him. For once he had taken matters into his own hands, determined to penetrate the city's humdrum surface in ways the desk dwellers upstairs wouldn't dare. It could lead nowhere. He was taking a leap without a net, and it made him giddy. And sure enough, eventually distant figures appeared on the island of yellow grass, trekking from the crossroads. He counted five. They went single file down the other side of the island into the murk before reappearing in the shade of the plane's upended tail. Several squatted as though over a game in the dirt.

The sun was fading. Garbage runs had ceased for the day, and whole families materialized around the roadside vendors, knocking down lean-tos and carting the pieces away, every old woman and barefooted kid with a chair or a bucket. They trooped westward away from the drifting smoke to the crossroads, leaving Spenser alone in the wasteland with the rootless boys.

When sunlight flashed off a pair of spectacles moving against the foot traffic he sensed that the pieces were falling into place. A bony old guy picked his way between the homebound families, moving into the haze and then down into the shadows among the street kids. A few minutes later the spectacles flashed back into view. Five heads came bobbing up onto the sunlit fringe of grass, trailing him towards the crossroads.

Back on the ground Spenser took the pistol from his map case. With shaking hands he inserted a magazine and jacked a round into the chamber. How the old pros would snicker: Check out the boy commando! Don't drop it on your foot!

He kicked his way through the tall grass. For sleeping quarters they had shipping cartons – Kelvinator and Speed Queen – with rags for blankets. Otherwise there wasn't much to see beyond the usual clouds of flies. Nothing of interest except, on second glance, a design scratched in the dirt – squares of various sizes arranged within a large rectangle in a pattern that was weirdly familiar to him. It was like a floor plan.

Strapped in beside the open door of a Huey climbing from Ton Son Nhut, off on yet another courier run, he had seen that same pattern over and over. From a bird's-eye view those squares were rooftops – corrugated metal on the outlying buildings, red tiles on the mansion in the center – and the rectangle containing them was a wall topped with concertina wire. Crudely laid out in the dirt at his feet was an overview of one of several US Army installations in the Tan Son Nhut neighborhood, a walled villa amid the grimy suburban sprawl. Probably the army had leased it from a dragon lady or Cholon millionaire as it had the villa in which Spenser's intelligence center was housed. It might have been the signal brigade headquarters or the logistics command or some other rear area nerve center. By helicopter it was just seconds from where he was standing. By taxicab, maybe ten minutes. He could not pull out now if he wanted to.

In bed that night he was so exhilarated by his discovery

that it took a while for him to detect a humming sound coming from the ceiling fan. But no, it was not the fan but the windows again. They were shivering. Was another ammo dump going up in flames? If so the explosions were too distant to be heard yet strong enough to rattle windows miles away. Probably they had infiltrated Bien Hoa or Long Binh again.

At the bus stop next morning the usual country voices traded bits of lifer chitchat. Such was the fraternity of senior NCOs. They complained about the windows, couldn't sleep, damn our little slant-eyed friends anyhow. Cigarettes were lit and there was much coughing and spitting into dust clouds rolling off the gravel road from Vietnamese litter jeeps barreling in from the countryside.

At the mess hall everyone had an opinion, but all they knew was that an ammo dump had been hit and Vietnamese casualties were pouring into town. A major at John's table shrugged it off as just another flare-up, no big deal, but he was a finance officer. What could a finance officer know about the enemy's intentions? John brooded over his scrambled eggs. Who would listen to his tale about a sketch in the dirt?

A work crew from the Long Binh stockade was manhandling desks down the stairwell. The halls were lined with padlocked file cabinets waiting their turn. Spenser went looking for his supervisor, a young captain famous for his surfer tan, but he was being mobbed by Vietnamese typists. "You no say nahthing!" one woman shrieked at him. "You jus' go 'way, you take ow wuk! Me madda, me fadda, me babysan..."

From the gravel terrace below the window came the voice of First Sergeant Rojo: "Listen up, gentlemen, for I have news for thee." A groan went up from the draftee clerks and technicians gathered for morning formation. They knew, and now Spenser knew as well. The dreaded day had come. Goodbye to the flesh pots of Saigon. Hello, Long Binh.

Spenser needed to talk. He tried his California captain first, trailing him from office to office, but the man avoided him, bounding ahead clutching a clipboard, driven by deadlines on his mimeographed schedule. Spenser looked for Major Francis, the installation commandant, and found him nose to nose with an officer from Plans and Programs, arguing about which section was responsible for transporting radio equipment. Spenser squeezed his way upstairs to the second story hoping to corner one of the analysts only to be met by a rush of fellow junior officers and turned back. They had been ordered back to the buses. They had an hour to pack up their personal gear. No one gave a damn about a second lieutenant with a theory.

Soon their bus was stuck in a barely oozing river of Vietnamese buses festooned with bicycles and baskets and white-knuckled hangers-on, plus Vietnamese army trucks heaped with women, kids, cooking utensils and mattresses. His fellow lieutenants were oblivious. They had napped on the ride to work. They were napping on the ride back to their quarters. They didn't care. They would wait this out. The decisive battle for Saigon could be shaping up all around them, but they cared only about getting their gear and their stereo systems stowed for the trip to the new place. He had news, damn it! Lives could be saved. It was as though the army was taunting him, reminding him again of how far outside the flow of significant events he was, stuck in a bus that was stuck in traffic.

Back in his room he went through the old panicky motions, jerking uniforms from hangers, tossing everything onto the bed, yanking open his duffel and jamming it full – boots, tent half, web gear, mess kit... He hated to pack, hated the training camp terror of falling behind, fucking up, drawing attention to himself. Even more he hated himself for doing this at all. He did it because he'd been ordered to do it, because everyone else was doing it, because it was his lifelong habit to go with the flow while secretly biding his time until... until what? In a frenzy he stuffed in mosquito netting, tent stakes, handfuls of underwear the color of mud.

Then he stopped. Rowdy banter echoed through the halls: "Ceramic elephants? Sure we'll help you stash 'em? Spread your cheeks!"

He sat on the bed, thinking.

Back on his feet he dug the map case from his footlocker, hitched it over his shoulder and headed down the back stairway.

The bus was crowded onto the sidewalk, idling. Spenser poked his head into the street, and smiling back at him around a perfumed cigarette was his scarecrow of a cyclo driver. He gunned the engine as though to say, 'Took you long enough!' Spenser climbed aboard and pointed. "Tan Son Nhut," he said.

His man was very good. He had an instinct for congestion in the making. Where gridlock congealed around a man face down on Cong Ly, spilled from a truck or a bus, he bumped up onto the sidewalk. He sped down terraces and dodged the slops tossed from second stories, dodged half-naked children picking through mounds of trash, dodged the bleating trucks and military vehicles. Out of the heart of the city he sped through one smoky, stunted crossroads community after another until, approaching the airbase, they entered a plume of red dust thrown up by an intersecting convoy, mostly flatbed trucks pulling shrouded howitzers. Soldiers in flak jackets sprawled among sandbags and timbers.

Once again traffic boxed them in, but his driver had a fury about being cornered, and he bullied his way to the side of the road and down a lane running parallel to the convoy. Between the flatbeds they sped past was a vehicle that reminded Spenser of the Good Humor trucks of his boyhood except it was painted green and bore the stenciled words, MORTUARY – DO NOT DELAY. Spenser's driver sped past the MP jeep leading the convoy and then cut in front, looping around it and speeding away through yet another boomtown neighborhood of cinderblock, plywood and tin. The big city press of machines and tempers fell away. Chickens strutted and pecked under lines of drying laundry, but there was not a human being in sight.

Spenser waved him to the side of the road where they poured over Spenser's map. Suddenly the scarecrow came to life, stabbing the map with a finger and jabbering. "No go! No go!" he said. He did a quick U-turn and sped back to the busy main road, Plantation Road they called it, and for the next twenty minutes he rumbled along more cautiously. Traffic thinned until they had a whole side of the road to themselves, with only an occasional military vehicle speeding by in the other direction. Eventually the driver pulled over beside empty tables of an outdoor cafe. He flapped his hand, waving into the distance and talking fast. As far as he was concerned this was the end of the line. Spenser paid up and watched him speed back to the city.

Alone in the quiet of an unfamiliar crossroads, Spenser imagined the other guys packed solid in their bus, walled in by duffel bags and packing cartons. Soon they would be setting up their hi-fis and ceramic elephants in brand-new quarters in a brand-new fortress-compound in Long Binh, out of harm's way for the duration.

He tucked the map case under his arm and set off jogging down the side road. He took comfort from the weight of the pistol.

The usual woebegone pups came sniffing around. A pot-bellied toddler standing in an open doorway watched him pass. Hands reached out and jerked the child back into the shadows. Shutters on both sides of the lane were being shut. A drumming sound overtook Spenser from behind, and he turned to discover a dirty grey wall of rain rushing over him. In a second the sour haze was washed from the air. He was soaked and chilled clean through.

He was looking for white masonry walls topped with concertina wire that he had seen from the air, but it was the gate that caught his eye – a dinged-up slab of black painted iron.

He pushed and it gave way. No guards, no barrier. He heard the crump, crump of explosions and the woodpecker tap of distant machine-gun fire. Probably they were probing the perimeter of the air base again. But then they were always going after Ton Son Nhut. He wished he had his radio. The military police net would be swarming, likewise the control towers. By now even the BBC might be shedding light on whether today's excitement was just routine harassment or the start of the long expected offensive.

He walked in unchallenged. From the helicopters he had grown used to seeing heatwaves rising from two huge engines in the generator shed, but the engines were gone. Nothing was left but oil stains. Sandbags were heaped in the corners of the wall where before there had been guard towers.

He went cautiously along the gravel drive, passing the guards' barracks and mess hall. The motor pool had reverted to a vacant yard. Vietnamese drivers used to nap on the back seats of jeeps there, and soldiers in jungle fatigues had criss-crossed the grounds of the compound carrying folders from one white building to another. Neighborhood kids might have been impressed by this mysterious enterprise, with its rifle-toting guards, vehicles of all kinds coming and going, and at night, the otherworldly moat of light encircling the place. But anyone who saw it from the air would have known immediately what went on here. Paperwork. Typewriters and telephones. Just another administrative headquarters.

Too timid to tap a busy captain on the shoulder and insist that he be heard, Spenser had been rash enough to plunge into no man's land and raise the alarm himself. Here he was, in sole possession of an abandoned US Army compound. In the battle of accelerating schedules – the other side's big push against Saigon versus our army's migration to Long Binh – he was an obvious loser.

He was mounting steps to the mansion's front porch when it occurred to him that he had not closed the gate. This was his first real scare. He reminded himself that open or closed the gate didn't matter anymore. The place was wide open regardless. They could come over the walls or through the motor pool. They could do anything they wanted.

The front door was unlocked. He eased it open and closed it behind him. Someone somewhere had a key, but meanwhile there was no way to lock it. Like his own outfit, they had pulled out in a hurry. You would expect a decent sweep and mop job at least, but the terrazzo floor was a mess of dusty boot prints and cigarette butts.

The emptiness spooked him enough to retrieve his pistol and chamber a round. It was an old, standard issue forty-five automatic, a brick with a trigger. He was a lousy shot, but the gun's weight alone was a confidence builder, a reminder that even in his shaky hand it could be a killer. He headed for the stairway, wet boots squishing with each step.

If this headquarters was like his own, in the early years of shortages and improvisation it would have been blessed with an old master sergeant and veteran scrounger who was forever turning up with the stuff they needed most – a refrigerator, a truck full of desks and typewriters left over from the Military Assistance Command era: toilet seats, cases of Shasta and San Miguel. Phase two would have been the great flood – equipment and soldiers pouring in faster than they could be sorted out and sent into the field, the swapping of cooks for wire splicers, personnel specialists for infantrymen. Now, on what might be shaping up as the first day of phase three, the final battle, he found himself alone in a deserted mansion just as all the army's scattered headquarters around Saigon were hauling ass to an isolated pre-fab city in the countryside where they would be safe behind minefields, wire, and patrolling tanks.

He wondered if here as at his headquarters a Cambodian maid with gold teeth had come clip-clopping up the stairs about this time of day cupping a fresh-cut pineapple in her hands, refreshment for the general. Where was she now, and on whose side?

Upstairs he passed through the outer office where clerks had shuffled paper, through the chief of staff's office, and into the room where flags and framed photos and citations had decorated the walls. The commanding general's office, now just an empty bedroom again.

At the window he watched a yellow dog lope through the gate, sniff sandbags and mark them, then wander back into the lane. It was strangely dark out there. He checked his watch. Still not quite four. He looked again. The second hand was not moving. In the excitement that morning he had forgotten to wind it.

He had to stay. You don't take to the streets just before nightfall. You find a corner and hunker down in your wet clothes. He had M&Ms and raisins in a plastic cigarette box and twelve rounds in two magazines, and he was coming down with a helluva case of the shakes.

The wide open gate was a concern. In the morning, sputtering vehicles of all kinds would crowd the lane, evidence of a normal day. He would wave down a passing jeep and all would be well, but for now that unsecured gate loomed large. This could be the night he became a minor item in the news.

Probably there was a toilet nearby, but he was reluctant to venture from his corner. From off in the distance came more spasms of automatic fire, then a flurry of explosions. Up in the shadows a lizard was impatient about something, like someone rapping a coin on a counter. He waited.

His ruminations were interrupted by light projected against the wall opposite the window. The light blinked off and on twice, as was the custom for military vehicles halting at a guarded entry.

They had come for him. That was his first thought. They had counted noses and come up one short. Go find Junior, they'd been told. So here they were, and so much for his plunge into history.

He came uncoiled from his corner and crawled to the back of the room, raising his head just enough to see over the sill. A small utility truck had stopped just inside the gate. He could imagine how pissed off they were at being sent on this goose chase in the first place, much less finding themselves detained at an empty guard post.

Where the hell was the guard to check them out and wave them in?

He was tempted to raise the window and shout: 'Wait up! I learned my lesson!' Anything to keep them from backing out and speeding away.

The truck lurched forward. Heading to the stairway he felt prickly, hot and giddy. He could not bring himself to go boldly out the front door, so he eased open the screen door at the base of the stairs and passed through a curtain of drizzle as he went down steps to the ground. He had an eerie sense that they were on foot looking for him. A sudden whack-whack of rotors thundered overhead. Flares popped and drifted down off in the direction of the airbase, illuminating a startlingly intricate pattern of boot and tire tracks in the gravel. Walls on all sides of the yard glowed Easter-egg pink.

He crept cautiously along the back of the building, stopped at the corner and peered around the edge. All clear. He started towards the front. A fluorescent glow glided over the beaten grass of the motor pool like a giant jellyfish. One more turn and he faced the front of the building. There, all was in darkness. He heard the truck's idling motor. As he crept closer he felt heat rising from the hood. He stepped carefully for fear of tripping over the steps to the front entry. Probably they were waiting at the door or had already gone inside.

That's when he detected a familiar scent – tobacco smoke, the perfumed Vietnamese kind. An arm's length away the pinpoint glow of a burning cigarette was reflected in a pair of spectacles.

The old man may have been waiting for his street commandos to reassemble at his side, or maybe he just wanted an explanation. After all that elaborate planning, after all the risks they had run, the compound was empty.

Spenser had to assume he had a weapon. It was a matter of getting off the first shot. He had no choice. As he extended his arm he felt the gun's muzzle bump something hard. Cheekbone? He had spent hours on the firing line, but that single explosion was the loudest sound he'd ever heard.

He ran, and he heard others running. What he needed was protection from falling debris. He dove under the roof of the generator shed and hit the deck. Someone dashed past on the gravel drive, heading out the gate. Another was right on his heels. It was as though he had stirred up a nest of them. How many skinny kids with satchel charges would fit in a little cargo truck? How many would they risk on a place like this?

The first to go up was the boxy two-story between the mansion and the volleyball court. Chunks of cement and stucco thudded on his steel roof. A glowing ball of dust rolled out of the darkness bringing a taste of metal. The next to blow was a flimsy tropical building, all wood strips and screening. It took forever for the debris to settle. Finally the truck exploded, collapsing the front wall of the mansion and sending another dust cloud over him. For a minute the only sound was the flutter of typing paper falling out of the sky.

Spenser always intended to find out if more bodies had been found in the rubble, but he never did. He was certain of only one, the old fellow with the bossy wife. Spenser kept pointing out to the MPs where the body was buried under tons of cinder block and plaster. He insisted that the man had not been killed by falling rubble but by one large caliber pistol round fired point-blank to the head. Spenser's mouth was caked with masonry dust. It was in his eyes. He was shrouded in it. He did not have himself under good control. He was just glad to see them, and he wanted them to know that he had not been hiding. He had been out in the middle of all this, playing a role in this story, for better or worse.

1989

———

Jack Hagan took the right-hand ramp back onto the interstate, heading north. Drumlin was where he'd grown up, done dumb things with long-term implications and still had lingering obligations, but Drumlin was south. Once again it was a name in *The Stalker* that had been on his mind and determined his direction.

As a junior at Drumlin High School in the late 1930s, Hagan had taken Industrial Arts from a teacher named Ernie Cornish, a hard-nosed guy with a sharp wit and a gift for connecting with smart alecks. The class met on the second floor where oak branches reached almost to the windows, and a pair of squirrels Mr Cornish had named Molly Cule and Aleck Tron perched on the outer sill, brazenly spying on them. Mr Cornish wielded a yardstick like a bull whip. His cure for rowdiness was to lash it against his desk. He meant business, but strangely his roomful of tough guys and show-offs seemed to like being treated like beasts of burden. He also happened to be famous as Captain Cornish, commander of a troop of horse cavalry known as Machine Gun Troop, and he always had an eye out for potential recruits. He wasn't after just anybody. If Mr Cornish took you aside after class and suddenly became Captain Cornish, recruiter, that was a very big deal.

One day in October the class was silenced not by the usual whack on the desk but by the clatter of hooves on the leaf-strewn street below. In no time the boys were crowding the windows. That swarm of manes and glistening flanks flowing by like rapids in a muddy river was new cavalry mounts for Machine Gun Troop of the 105th Cavalry Regiment, Cornish explained. They had just arrived at the station and were heading for stables on the edge of town. When the horses were gone, Jack turned from the window and saw Cornish standing behind his desk, smiling. Cornish met his gaze with a wink and a nod.

It was a recruiting gimmick, of course. Cornish had arranged for the horses to put on the same show every year, though young troopers were already in uniform before they learned from the stable sergeant that they had been conned. By then they had survived an unofficial initiation – manure fights and so-called 'saddle fittings' that left a guy sprawled on his back staring at his horse's belly. The stable sergeant, a full-timer named Rooney, loved horses but wasn't so sure about people in general and new recruits in particular. "Talk to 'em. Let 'em know you're here," he growled at newcomers pussyfooting through the stables.

Then one evening in November, Hagan found himself in the middle of a mounted column, descending into a valley of scrub oak and sand, sloshing eastward across Otter Creek, on patrol with the United States Cavalry. His sense of what war was like came from picture book images of civil war carnage and the shattered moonscapes of the Western Front. In his mind, battle consisted of uniformed mobs converging amid explosions overhead and underfoot. But the patrol he rode out on that chilly night was from an earlier world – creaking leather, snorting mounts, night air laced with pine.

Captain Cornish insisted that even in the era of trucks and armored tanks horse soldiers would remain the eyes and ears of the infantry, in constant motion beyond the mass of advancing foot soldiers, sending back information about enemy movements. Machine Gun Troop's additional job was to provide fire support to cover the infantry's flanks. Horses were their mobility and water-cooled Browning machine guns were their firepower.

Each squad worked on a noisy, blazing, tour-de-force drill that brought a thrill to crowds at county fairs. It was a hundred-yard, tight formation gallop that ended with the gunner swooping from his McClellan saddle to lay ahold of the Browning hooked to the pack horse alongside, while on the other side of the pack horse his assistant unhooked the tripod. All six men pulled up short, swung to the ground at the same time and went to work – gathering the horses, opening a canister and lifting out a belt of ammunition, fitting gun to tripod – until the gunner loosed a burst into the ground. There was something about the sound of a machine-gun squad galloping by that electrified a crowd. Partly it was the soundtrack thunder of tight-packed hooves, but there was a clatter and crash of metal as well, and the orchestration of those sounds along with a snap vision of grimacing, dust-eating troopers bent low over a blur of mane had a way of sending a chill down your spine, as though Righteous Victory itself had just flashed by, and your chest swelled with pride knowing that the good old US of A had nothing to fear from those strutting show-off armies in the newsreels.

Little did those civilians know that most of the noise was provided by rocks jumping around in empty ammunition canisters.

For Hagan it was great fun even though he was too much of a tenderfoot to participate in the fancy stuff – Roman riding, pony express races, mounted wrestling or precision demonstrations of the walk, trot and canter. Like other newbies from Industrial Arts he had a lot to learn but not enough time to learn it.

Through it all, Captain Cornish was that special guy, master organizer, trainer, horseman and leader, the first to arrive and last to go home, the guy who did more push-ups, sit-ups, and pull-ups than kids half his age. He never seemed to tire, and even if his back was turned he knew if you screwed up, fell short, or tried to cheat, and he was in your face in a flash. You would be a fool not to take that big toothy grin seriously.

Of course it all turned out to be a fairy tale – the moonlit patrols, the sense of an urgent mission should war come, the horses-forever mystique – but that only came to light gradually.

By the summer of 1940, western Europe had fallen

to the Nazis and the Battle of Britain was on. In August a division of the regular army took over a nearby county along with platoons of new tanks. Flights of bombers and fighter planes appeared overhead. Tent cities blossomed on farm fields and long convoys of army trucks stirred up dust on county roads. Machine Gun Troop and all the other units of the Bold Eagle division from across the state were drawn into the big green machine. The first major war games since World War One were underway, and for all the noise and excitement overhead and erupting from distant woodlands and hills, there wasn't much for Jack Hagan and his fellow troopers to do except tend the horses. They ended up on work details everyone else was too busy to do like gathering wood for field kitchens.

Then one afternoon they were roused from their slumbers and sent galloping off to protect the flank of Blue forces. But as soon as they arrived they were ruled out of action by the umpire on the scene. Half-tracks scouting in advance of the Orange attackers had gotten there first and cut them to notional ribbons with their own machine guns. The troop's only other critical mission took place on a rainy night when they were sent off to locate a series of landmarks that represented make-believe tactical headquarters, but Captain Cornish and the regular army major accompanying him spent much of the night scowling over a state highway map lit by flashlight. For all his compass-reading and pathfinding skills, Cornish and his staff failed to find even one of the landmarks. The troopers plodded on hopelessly lost. The major was not impressed.

Yet Cornish remained their inspiration and guiding light when, two months later, the division was activated for federal service. By then Machine Gun Troop had been converted to a rifle company, its mounts shipped off to God knows where.

After months of training on fundamentals in Louisiana, the division joined an even more elaborate series of war games that lasted throughout the summer and fall of 1941, a wide-ranging motorized affair spread over three states. L Company, as the former troopers were now designated, spent most of their days eating dust and looking out of the back of canvas-covered trucks and sleeping rough in the field. It was a big deal just to sneak off to a roadside stand for a cold Coke. They had no idea what was going on and no longer heard from the leader who had always looked so impressive in T-shirt and trooper hat, the guy they would have followed into hell if he told them to, Captain Ernest Cornish, their link to high school and night patrols on horseback and a simpler world.

Rumor was he had been assigned to a rear area unit with other older captains and lieutenants. L Company's new CO was a transfer from an outfit overstocked with eager-beaver young lieutenants. Youth had become all important. In strenuous leadership positions, especially when the going got tough, you needed hard-charging, hot-blooded youth. Everybody knew that.

L Company spent over a year in the deep south training for motorized maneuver warfare in Europe, and even as they headed west by troop train, expecting to embark for somewhere in the Pacific, few of the Drumlin originals could remember their new commander's name. They had yet to learn that none of their training over the past year and a half had prepared them for what lay ahead.

Jack had never been crazy about horses and their upkeep, but he sure missed those early years of playing cavalry trooper under Ernie Cornish, the coolest teacher and best friend a teenager could have in addition to being a hard ass spine-straightener, attitude adjuster and spirit-lifter. It wasn't right that he'd been shunted aside before the Ponga campaign. No one would have choked up and abandoned their weapons if he'd still been in charge, Hagan believed. No one would have malingered behind the lines. Captain Cornish would have explained what was going on, made sense of their situation, and led from the front.

A brief message about him in *The Stalker* had been on Hagan's mind. It had been written by his son. *My father, Ernie Cornish, is failing and troubled in mind. Kind thoughts from any who served with him in Machine Gun Troop would be deeply appreciated.*

Troubled in mind. That was not the Ernie Cornish that Hagan remembered. He had never been much of a hand-holder, but he would gladly reach out to his old captain while there was still time.

Kaunaukee was up in musky country, the big woods, land of the lumber barons. Cornish had been somewhat of a celebrity in Drumlin. At a time when regular army soldiers ranked with hobos in the public's mind and had to scrape by on leftovers from the last war, Cornish was the image of military pride, vigor and competence. Why would he ever leave a town that looked up to him for an out of the way place like Kaunaukee?

By mid-afternoon, fields of drying corn gave way to piney hills and flashing bodies of water. Hagan's family had never been north country adventurers. Their crowd didn't have money for tourist cabins and fancy lodges. No summers at the beach for them.

Not much was doing at the A&W in the village of Grantly. A sign was propped in the window of *Annie's Homemade Fudge*: SEE YOU NEXT SUMMER.

Kaunaukee, an hour later, was a real town built on an isthmus between a pair of lakes. He drove through blocks of tourist shops and saloons and an adjacent neighborhood of weary little houses with neglected yards. The new money was in the lake-front chalets he caught sight of while driving uphill into a densely shaded community of old money estates. Once upon a time these hills and all the land around had been a universe of tree stumps as far as the eye could see, but oaks and maples had long since filled in for the harvested pines.

It was common knowledge that Cornish's wife had money, so Hagan wasn't surprised that the address given in *The Stalker* was in the same neighborhood where lumber barons had put up their fussy Victorians. In fact the Cornish place proved to be a relatively modest affair of brick and timbers and moss-eaten shingles.

No one came to the door. Through a back porch window Hagan saw wicker furniture and dead plants aligned on a bookcase. A scent from out of the past lured him down to the shore a few lots over. Burning leaves. An old-timer was standing guard with a rake.

"She's been gone for years," the man told him, "but Ernie carried on as long as he could. These old places keep you busy. There's always something needs fixing, which seemed to suit a hyper guy like him. But no, his son finally had to move him into the Lighthouse."

At the Lighthouse Senior Living Center, a short and very pregnant woman came out of an office behind the front desk and introduced herself. The name was Tao or Dao. "I have to ask who you are and the purpose of your visit," she told Jack.

Hagan didn't mind. They were looking out for their residents. Here she was, a young woman light years from the land she came from, now a social worker concerned with the welfare of an elderly client.

He told her about his history with Captain Cornish, and she led him down a long hallway. "We've had issues with some of his visitors. If he's willing to see you, you can visit briefly, but I'll have to sit in." She turned onto another hallway. Doors were bedecked with crêpe-paper pumpkins and other autumn ornamentation. She greeted by name the old-timers passing by in wheelchairs or behind walkers.

At Cornish's door she knocked, waited a moment, then went in and shut the door behind her. A minute later she waved Jack in.

A few shirts and pants hung in the closet. The window across the room offered a view of a parking lot and fenced off trash bins. A thirsty-looking pair of potted plants stood on the sill. On the bedside table stood a framed family photo, the captain in dress uniform with his wife on one side, two grown sons on the other. Centered high up on the opposite wall was a television set fitted to a platform. A long life of hard-won achievements was stripped down to this.

He was sitting up in bed dressed in a sort of gym suit, yet his ancient face was aglow with anticipation – a welcoming, quizzical sort of smile and enormous sparkling eyes like a glimpse into deep space. He might have been smiling in a receiving line, greeting old soldiers he hardly recognized anymore. He offered a trembling hand and said, strangely, "Yes!"

Hagan took his hand but was suddenly tongue-tied. From her chair in the corner Mrs Tao whispered, "Tell him who you are."

Hagan introduced himself. "I was one of your students half a century ago, then one of your troopers. Here I am, still flustered as hell just being in the same room with you, Captain. I was one of the punks you shaped up back in the days of Machine Gun Troop, when you meant the world to us."

"Yes," Cornish said again.

Jack loosened his grip, and Cornish's hand dropped to the bed. "I live in Australia now. My life turned out so different from what I expected, so much better. I owe that to you, Captain. If not for you I'd still be a sourpussed punk hanging out on the streets of Drumlin."

"Yes," Cornish said. "I didn't know... I didn't know then..."

"I think about those evening patrols, what magic they were. I guess it's safe now for me to admit that I never was much of a horseman. Such big teeth. Such nasty hooves. But I would have mounted a tiger if that's what it took to ride with you and to call you my commander. We all felt that way, you know. Couldn't admit it of course, but we did."

"That's very nice, isn't it, Ernie?" Mrs Tao said. "Mr Hagan has fond memories! He admires you still for so many years! His whole life, even! That's very nice for you!"

"Yes, but I didn't know..."

"I was like you," Hagan went on. "I expected to go off and defend the beaches or crawl through the jungle with L Company, but at the last minute I got reassigned. I spent the war behind a typewriter in Melbourne. Can you believe that? I didn't ask for it, didn't even want it, but like you I missed the big show—"

"I had nothing to do with it!" Cornish shouted, seeming to back away. "That's the truth, damn it! I keep telling people but they blame me anyway."

Mrs Tao cast a troubled glance at Hagan. He tried again: "Sir, I just came by to wish you well and let you know I'll never forget those years with you. I'm Jack Hagan, one of your former troopers and many admirers."

"Yes, sure, I know what you think, but I couldn't help it. I couldn't know. No one did back then."

"Okay, Ernie," Mrs Tao said. She moved forward to pat his hand. "Okay. You rest now. We'll let you be."

Back in the hallway Hagan shook his head, bewildered. "I don't get it. We loved the guy. What did I do wrong?"

She was stomping down the hall ahead of him. "We try everything to make peace for him, but he goes on like that – like he's haunted, poor man."

1988

L ATE ON A FRIDAY AFTERNOON AT MCCOY Barracks in Stuttgart, John Spenser lounged at his desk pondering a problem that had nothing to do with the shambles spread out before him – stacks of coded printouts which, properly interpreted, might reveal something significant about the other side, plus memos, regulations, photocopies of photocopies, all of which the bronze light of late afternoon had transformed into something archaic – unearthed shards and tools to be indexed, catalogued and shelved out of sight. Through his nearly twenty years at this desk he had been tormented by a vague suspicion that somewhere in that mess was a buried urgency that he couldn't face, and that it was ticking down to a terrible outcome. Only recently he had discovered that it was not on his desk but buried in his head.

He was stuck. He had taken a wrong turn. Something fundamental had dried up and fallen away. He had spent his youth marking time, waiting for his chance to become one of those solitary lookouts prowling the old world for ominous signs in the closing of certain borders, the silencing of certain figures, and the flare-up of long-buried grievances. He would disappear behind the Iron Curtain where developments of great interest to the west were hidden behind a smokescreen of propaganda: smiling student gymnasts performing for old men looking down from on high; lines of 'citizens' waiting to cast their votes for the only candidate. He would speak their languages. He would seek out the renegades and malcontents biding time in grubby, purgatorial anonymity. In time, certain truths vital to our side or to him personally would reveal themselves.

After his discharge from the army he landed a position as a civilian analyst in army intelligence. It was what he had been preparing for all his life. He was on his way. More years of training and apprenticeship followed until finally orders came assigning him to where he felt he belonged, up against the dark menace of the Iron Curtain.

Yet here he was in his late-forties still chained to a desk and for what?

As usual this late in the day, the office was empty. Copy machines were still. Microfiche files padlocked, computer terminals dead. Corridors that had echoed with jackboots half a century ago were lined with cartons of computer paper and watercolors from the army's combat artist program. His fourth-story dormer in this old Wehrmacht kaserne poked from a steeply pitched roof up among the wildlife in the trees. Far below and a half block down the road, young soldiers poured from the commissary like looters, twelve packs on their shoulders. This was their last weekend for pizza, cold beer, and a roof over their heads. On Monday they would set off in convoys for the woods and marshes of the Luneburg Heath, home of Britain's Army of the Rhine, for autumn war games.

His section had occupied these offices ever since the world all around was rubble and broken people stooped under the weight of rubble and little trains set up to haul that rubble away from the gutted city. Worker ants in tattered clothes chipped mortar from bricks and stacked them in the pale hope that a city might rise again. The survivors had moved underground. Bomb shelters had become apartment complexes. A subterranean hotel operated under the ruined Markplatz. Over it all lingered smoke and grit and the stink of the unwashed.

By the time Spenser joined the office, the surrounding hills were once again a realm of gardens and gracious living. The streets of the rebuilt city below smelled of perfume and spicy meats introduced by guest workers from the Middle East.

To a visitor, the office he worked in might appear to be a permanent fixture, as eternal as a bank or a church, but in fact they never expected to survive the next budget cycle. Teams of men in suits dispatched by an inspector general or a congressional committee or the Government Accountability Office were forever poring over their records. Like his fellow analysts, Spenser suspected that one day they would find what they were looking for: the work done here was redundant, it cost too much, or they had screwed up in some unforgivable way. In the back of their minds they always expected to be vaporized in the next budget.

The rumors didn't bother their section chief. "They can't send us home," he insisted. "They don't have any place to put us." He was a plum-shaped fellow with a vaguely art-world air. He wore knit ties and pastel shirts. Mortality weighed heavily on him: sinus headaches, seasonal allergies, and the burden of deadlines. Fridays he was out the door by two o'clock. You would think he had emerged from a marathon debriefing, but in fact he had been hanging out in the cafeteria and the mailroom, carrying on about the ringing in his wife's ears. Damn it, if army doctors couldn't find out what was wrong he'd find a German who could. Spenser watched him amble to his Volvo station wagon, sunglasses perched atop his curly head, hands deep in the pockets of a leather flight jacket. Spenser was certain he was calculating time in grade, pension points, and years, months, weeks to retirement.

The second in command was married to a diplomat. She got the job because she was well connected. She made no bones about it. She had some kind of clinical degree and told Spenser that she was administering a program that had something to do with profiling mid-level players on the other side: "If I told you more, I'd have to shoot you." She made a great display of taking work home and persevering in the face of adversity. She always came in late. Her leather handbag crashed on her desk, and her million-dollar hair and bloodshot eyes appeared over the top of his cubicle wall. She was upset about her son Phineas, or Finny as she called him, who was such a free spirit his prep school teachers back home didn't know what to make of him.

This was not the mysterious and tantalizing Europe of Spenser's dreams. Far from haunting the dark side of the Iron Curtain, he was living in comfort and spending his days in a cubicle in a building full of Americans in cubicles. Every now and then in the evening after an extra mug of Pilsner he would walk back to his apartment sniffing the air for perfumed cigarette smoke. If only he could have gotten to know that old taxi driver he'd left buried under the rubble. He imagined the guy was nearby searching for him. He wanted to talk, and so did Spenser. If only they could settle in a booth together and drink and talk the night away, all would be well between them.

And then there was Mrs Neumann. For years she had been just a pleasant vision projected like an inflight movie across the humdrum stretches of his day. Only recently had she taken up residence inside him, occupying him totally like a fever or a crime. A daydream trained to curl at his feet now roamed the woods and grew claws.

At the end of the work day she had appeared below his window in a lavender raincoat. The passenger door of a black Mercedes opened from within. She cocked her head to greet the driver. People who speak a language you do not understand seem always to be on intimate terms. Spenser was certain she entered the car talking. She would be emphatic and a little breathless.

Mrs Neumann worked with Mr Mayer in the German liaison office two floors down. They translated stories about the other side that appeared in the German press. Every morning Spenser stopped at her desk to pick up the file. A week ago she had broken with routine and taken him to a room filled with old men in tweed suits and forest green vests and a few old women as well, with corsages and fussy hats. Their hands were busy with demitasse cups and pastries. The room was filled with high-spirited chatter. Waiters circulated with trays, and there was stringed music.

"They're so *cute!*" she whispered. "Don't you think? We don't forget our old spies. Every now and then, a little reunion. A discreet thank you from the agency."

Those relics would have been among the uprooted young recruited from Displaced Person camps and POW camps after the war, the Gehlen organization's first wave sent behind the Iron Curtain. They were the ones who had made it back to our side. The rest died sending numbers and gossip on poison pill transmitters, or they still moldered in East German prisons, waiting to be swapped. Eerie to think what those old-timers had been up to twenty or thirty years ago – who they were rubbing out or stealing blind. Now they needed help lighting cigarettes and being guided to the bathroom, while our army's new electronic spies – satellites, antennas, and computer banks – buried analysts like himself under more numbers and images than they could dig themselves out of.

Like the data gathered by Spenser's section, the news clips Mrs Neumann translated would be reduced to numbers and inserted into charts on overhead transparencies for the corps commander's five o'clock briefing, after which the documents from which the transparencies had been distilled would disappear into the shredder and the burn box. It was all reduced to numbers. Strength estimates, troop movements and intangibles converted to codes: alcohol consumption plus desertion rates plus summary discipline equals morale; manpower turmoil plus equipment shortages plus morale equals readiness, and so on. No ghostly border jumpers showed up in their offices to spill twenty years of accumulated secrets. It was all numbers now, stacks and stacks of them. Distill, Distribute, Destroy. That was their unofficial motto.

The old faces interested Spenser only because they interested her. They had worked together for years but he still didn't know anything about her. Did she have children? Did she love her husband? Above all, was she on to him? He was certain he had left clues – too many coincidental encounters in the mail room and cafeteria – and that in showering him with fleeting little intimacies she had been sending signals of some kind. Again and again she had grasped his arm as if on the verge of a breathless confession, only to be distracted at the last moment. With her broad shoulders and long limbs she called to mind those proud, strutting blondes of the old propaganda films, but unlike them, her face – at least whenever he ran into her – seemed alight with anticipation and good cheer, or so it had struck him. She was always kind of breathless in her bright colors and noisy shoes. He wondered if the opportunity to dress well had come to her late in life. In meetings she was forever taking stock, pulling at earrings, checking the fit of her rings and jangling her bracelets. She searched out loose threads and dealt with them mercilessly. Sometimes he caught her in a great unsuppressed yawn, other times impatiently examining her nails. Once, remarkably, she fixed him with a lingering moonbeam gaze.

He had become a hopeless case. That vision of a figure in lavender vanishing into the black Mercedes would be his last glimpse of her for three weeks. Or so he assumed.

* * *

Monday was misty and dim, the Germany of his schoolboy imagination. He spent most of it tucked between a green convoy of Canadian communication vans and the green convoy of an American army field bakery. All were headed north to the woods and marshes and sprawling farm fields of the Luneburg Heath. The scenario of this fall's maneuvers was the opening days of World War Three, a massive armored assault from the east. Spenser no longer had much to do at these affairs. He used to deliver the so-called 'Samson' disks to Orange Ops and Blue Ops each morning. It had seemed such a big deal back then, top secret stuff and all that, but two years ago the Samson disks had been done away with, so he had a lot of idle time on his hands. Still, he could not imagine missing the autumn wargames even though he sometimes felt like a piece of unclaimed luggage.

He had another job at the maneuvers, and it had become his only excuse for continuing to show up. It too was hush-hush, just not such a big deal. The maneuvers showcased the West's latest weapons systems – just the sort of thing the other side would love to know more about. So when 'reporters' showed up at the press center flashing business cards from obscure offices in Helsinki or Beirut or wherever, it was his responsibility to file that information for future reference. It was why he spent so much time at the copy machine duplicating forms for his boss's filing cabinet back in Stuttgart.

Late that afternoon he signed into the press center. The canteen was empty. The big room beyond where media representatives from NATO armies had their desks was also mostly empty, including the American desk. But Colonel Gert Ritter was back at the Bundeswehr desk, absorbed in a *Word Perfect* text, and so was the hard-drinking Belgian colonel whose name he could never remember. He was bellowing into his field phone – "Allo! Allo!" – still trying to connect with units out in the woods and meadows and still coming up short, just like last year.

Spenser's cubicle was through the press briefing room with its wall-sized maps of the maneuver area, in an out of the way corner of the Press Inquiries office. He was hard to find on purpose. Stay out of the traffic flow, keep your head down, don't speak up, seek invisibility, and mellow out in the comfort of the Cold War state of mind: watch towers, mined borders, our spies vs their spies, miles and miles of armor tucked out of sight, everyone primed for the balloon to go up, stand-off as a way of life.

For a few months of the year German reservists rotated through the old Luftwaffe camp, and for a few months the Brits settled in, but year-round the base was mostly empty, fogged-over and visited by roaming bands of wild pigs. Here, where the press would gather, the installation had the inoffensive look of an elementary school, generic and harmless. Nothing to provoke old memories.

He drove to a nearby crossroads village of half-timbered relics earth-colored with age. He had forgotten the nights here, how early they came on and how silent and heavy with mist was the darkness. His usual room at the gasthaus was waiting for him. He opened the dormer window and dug a briar pipe that had belonged to his grandfather from a pocket in his army field jacket. Jacket and pipe spent the rest of the year in the trunk of his car. The new tin of tobacco from which he filled the pipe would go in the trash bin when the maneuvers ended. He lit up and savored the old sweet melancholy. He was back.

At 0600 the next morning he joined the queue outside the mess hall listening to the British kitchen crew bellow insults at one another. A half hour later he was stacking books on his desk in his isolated cubicle. Decades ago he had rescued them from his grandfather's bedroom – *Across the Frontiers* by Philip Gibbs, *Black Lamb and Grey Falcon* by Rebecca West, *World Diary 1929-1934* by Quincy Howe, and so on – and on this rainy morning he chose Gibbs, drawn to the grieving Europe of the of the post-Great War era with its portents of even darker times to come. This was as close as he would ever get to being the lone wolf operative of his teenage dreams. He would never be sent over the border to haunt the chancelleries and cafes of gritty eastern cities where the old channels had closed down and the tattoo of cleated boots had replaced the peacetime shudder of collapsing umbrellas, never speed through a land with a treaty imposed name and peer out the train window at blurring trees and something awful beyond them that would change his life. Such were the visions revived by his grandfather's books.

"So, where do you fit in?"

He spun his chair and faced a woman wearing the army's new black sweater. Pinned to its epaulettes were the silver leaves of a lieutenant colonel. She was offering her hand. "Wanda Krueger," she said. "Just in from Frankfurt. I'm your American desk this fall. Making rounds, meeting folks while there's still time."

Spenser allowed his hand to be gripped. He had the presence of mind to say, "I'm not a player."

"But what do you do? I need to get a sense of who does what."

"I'm out of the loop," he said. "I'm not here."

"So, you must be the guy from Stuttgart. I heard about you. I think I might have a job for you." And off she went on her rounds.

His face burned. These middle-aged careerists didn't understand how essential it was for him to remain disengaged and out of the picture. It was why he hid out and why he armed himself with a briefcase and a worried look. He knew about women in black sweaters. In college they had staked out a table in the student union and brooded over the *Times* crossword puzzle. If a careless male ventured too close, heads shot up, challenging. Who are you and what are you doing here? Justify yourself.

Wanda Krueger. As though how he spent his time was any of her business. He grabbed a file and stalked to the mailroom to kill time at the duplicating machine.

He had already run off more forms than he'd need and was banging away at the stapler when the machine he had just abandoned hummed to life again and the scent of lilacs washed over him.

"Yeah, me too, Johnny," Mrs Neumann said, feeding forms of her own into the machine. "Copies, copies, copies. Already this morning reporters are bunching at the registration table. Hear their leper bells? One bus only so far."

He stared, enchanted: "Mrs Neumann! What a surprise!"

"For you maybe, but for me not so much, having to come all this way to the war nonsense. But we do what we're told, huh? Like the soldiers." She reached out and gave his stapler hand a squeeze. "At least I find here my old pal Johnny from work."

She was right. The press center was surging to life. Television crews and print reporters circulated among the national desks in search of stories, and the Press Inquiry people put down their *Stars and Stripes* to work the phones. Spenser wandered among the national desks collecting papers and then assembling and alphabetizing them at his desk. It was auto-pilot stuff – all he was capable of under the lingering influence of his mailroom encounter.

At the end of the day he was working his way through the mobbed canteen looking forward to a solitary walk to the gasthaus when a voice called, "Johnny! Come! Sit!"

To make room for him in the booth Mrs Neumann set in motion a domino effect, bumping butts with the gaunt figure of Wanda Kreuger who in turn compelled Major McNair of the British desk to move to the other side of the booth beside Colonel Ritter.

He was stunned by his good fortune. Her flesh pressed against his flesh. They were so close that her scent survived even the assault of Ritter's cigar. She was bright and giddy in a schoolgirl way in spite of the smoke and noise and table full of beer bottles and whisky tumblers.

"We are spies together, Johnny and I," she said by way of introducing him. She even slid her arm under his and squeezed. "We got all the secrets, don't we, Johnny?"

He was speechless.

"We're all fessing up here," Wanda Krueger said. "Sharing backgrounds. Colonel Ritter was just about to tell me what a Gepard is."

"Approach me from the east in a MIG," he said, waving the cigar, "and you will find out more about the Gepard than you want to know. We are air defense, lightning fast guns on a tank body. We hide in the forests. Our radar detects you through the mist before you know we exist, and we hose you out of the sky."

He rhapsodized about life stripped down to essentials. His people were the eyes and ears of the northern border, modern day Teutonic Knights, ears pricked to the braying horns of the eastern hordes. "Prussia lives on, you know. It is a state of mind. Born to kill, you might say. Ha ha."

Spenser was so delirious to find himself, out of the blue, in hip to hip, arm in arm proximity with Mrs Neumann that the tart tone of her response to Ritter, in rat-a-tat German, shocked him. This was not the giddy schoolgirl speaking. Ritter snapped back, and they erupted in a flurry of tongue-lashings. "Not all Germans feel this way," she said finally, blushing and sending up vapors of lilac-scented anxiety. Next thing Spenser knew, her clinging arm had become all elbow. She virtually manhandled him in her rush to get away, trembling in anger and abandoning him to the tender mercies of this strange American female and her apparent admirers.

Ritter seemed to sense his discomfort. Unlike most NATO officers in baggy off-the-shelf battle dress, he wore tailored dress greys, and unlike the pinned-on status ribbons of the mass production armies, his ribbons and rank were embroidered in gold-framed shadow boxes on his chest and lapels. You would expect a monocle and a disdain for riffraff like Spenser, but instead he beamed as though to a warrior knight like himself press duty was a lark – a chance to play the charming outlaw. He blew a smoke ring and winked at Spenser through the cloud, as though they were in cahoots: "Bavarians! To a Prussian, a Bavarian is a cross between an Austrian and a human being."

Spenser didn't get it. Was he being ridiculed? Was Mrs Neumann?

"I think we're getting a little far afield," Wanda Krueger said, "but I'm so glad I've gotten to know something about all of you. Even you." She was looking at Spenser. "What is your name again? Oh yes, you're one of our Seventh Corps spooks. I still have no idea what you're doing here."

He didn't take the bait. "We've been through that already," he said.

"I think I have a job for you. Wolfe and Stone. You must know them."

He shook his head. "That's not my line. I'm not a press escort."

"But you're a perfect fit. From what I've been told they

need an old hand who can beat them at their game, not some poor lieutenant," she said, dismissing twenty years of standard procedure. "People say they eat junior officers for lunch. Anyhow" – she lifted a briefcase to her lap – "see you bright and early." She too made a quick exit and was followed by Colonel Ritter who in parting threw up his hands in mock distress, still the joker.

Too late to be heard, Spenser said, "Out of the question."

Major McNair tossed down the last of his drink. "So, Johnny, how about our Prussian friend?" He was getting to his feet. "Hail fellow and all that, but we don't forget, do we?"

All night he paced his room. This was as far as he would get. So much for sneaking over borders, midnight parachute jumps, lone wolf anything. All he had to look forward to was duplicating machines and long days at a messy desk. This was his *life* for Christ's sake, and it was a mockery. Why had that awful female chosen him to torment? What had she discovered about him that he did not want to know about himself?

* * *

In the briefing room next morning Colonel Ritter loomed over the microphone and gave it a heroic puff. "*Guten tag!* Welcome to day one of Operation Northern Storm, NATO's corps-on-corps free-play field training exercise..." He was in his glory as his pointer danced over the map from symbol to symbol, laying out the scenario. At 0300 hours German border police had detected the massing of Orange forces across the border...

Spenser and Major McNair were trapped in a corner at the back of the crowded room. The air was thick with wet wool and tobacco breath. Spenser found it hard to breathe. "Your boys are in here somewhere," McNair said.

"My boys?"

"Wolfe and Stone, of course. No doubt set on cranking out another coffee table album of tanks poking their sexy tubes through the bushes. Lots of muddy young studs lolling around the field. Remember when our red-blooded countrymen preferred nekkid ladies? Those were the days."

But when the briefing ended it was Wanda Kreuger who caught Spenser's eye. Media people were pouring out of the room, and she stood like a rock in the rapids crying out above the pandemonium, "The bus to helicopters touring the battlefield will depart in exactly seven minutes! A box lunch will be provided. There are still vacancies aboard transports destined for interviews with American women in the field and a Patriot missile installation..." She had seized the arm of a hairy fellow draped with cameras. A second slouching fellow similarly burdened stood beside him. Wolfe and Stone. But Wanda Kreuger's laser gaze was fixed on Spenser. Her message was clear: I have corralled your beasts. Now deal with them. The dreaded confrontation was at hand.

Hours later, rain still fell but the gloom in Spenser's heart had lifted. In the marktplatz of a village just minutes from the East German border he and his two

Neanderthals lingered over steaming wedges of pizza and cold bottles of Flemsburger, and Spenser tried to recall what he'd been so upset about. This was fun! Escort duty with the notorious Wolfe and Stone had turned out to be no big deal after all. Convoy after convoy of armored vehicles groaned through the narrow streets under a kerosene-scented haze. His charges were after establishing shots: brutish machines framed by church steeples, slate roofs, and medieval profiles grinning from brick walls. Wolfe sat Indian style on the top of their green Chevy four-by-four while Stone braced himself against the polished snout of a playground dolphin. They wore military mix and match, tiger-striped cargo pants, mud-colored sweaters and vests swarming with pockets and gizmos. They were unshaven and grimy, expressionless as radar screens. Wolfe, the little one, was a talker. He was nostalgic about tanks. Any encounter with an older model was like running into a grade school friend. He loved M-60s, but loved M-48s even more, and he spotted them even though nowadays they were outfitted with Gatling guns or radar antennas instead of cannons. They weren't fussy about where their work showed up, whether on Japanese calendars or in a family of French slasher magazines filled with images from the days of empire – dead Arabs, Vietnamese, and blacks, and Legionnaires beating the bush for rebels in God knows where. Their photos also appeared in special issues for World War Two sentimentalists – flying fortresses at sunset, Sherman tanks in a flowery meadow, overweight re-enactors pausing for a cigarette break.

Later, butting up against each other in the doorway of a Blackhawk helicopter, Wolfe and Stone aimed their cameras at massive new Abrams battle tanks stopped at the side of a road, sheets of plastic spilling placenta-like from open hatches. Sodden figures huddled on the ground beside them. The big eyes of their gasmasks gazed back at the photographers hanging from the sky. Nearby, cows huddled around an ancient bathtub in the mud. Spenser sagged against his sling seat feeling a deep sense of relief. They were decent enough guys after all. Everything was under control.

Such ups and downs. Such excitement. These runaway moods were making him light-headed. Last night – hounded, trapped, counting down the hours to disaster. Today – reprieve, exhilaration, good will to all. Such were his reflections in the mailroom later as he ran registration forms through the copy machine. Just then Mrs Neumann rushed in wide-eyed and flush-faced, shaking rain from her hair and chattering high-speed German at the soldier behind the counter.

"So this is where you hide away," she said. "You are not at your desk, not in the canteen. All day you are missing, and now I know."

Her brightness disoriented him, the glow of her skin and her lavender raincoat, the nervous energy of her voice. What he said surprised even him: "You're working too hard. Come escape with me to the old Sergeants' Club."

"Yes, sure, easy for you," she said, "but the papers don't translate themselves."

"I'll tell you what's in the papers. It's raining. The roads are full of side-lined tanks and wet soldiers. You know it all already."

"But my boss is waiting for the afternoon editions. Always rush, rush..." She hesitated and looked at him with a puzzled expression. She said something to her soldier, and he put down the stack of papers he had been holding for her. "Only a little break then," she said.

The moment they stepped outside Spenser knew he had a problem. There was no way she could walk to the club, not in those shoes. His car was back at the gasthaus. He tagged along as she dug through her bag for keys and led him to a sporty little Opal rental. Never in his daydreams of sneaking away with her had she been the driver.

She drove crowding the wheel and squinting through the sweeping wipers. "So, will the battle be over tomorrow, do you think?" she asked. "They say the tanks tear up the fields."

Pines and alders blurred past his window, nature reclaiming an old runway built by slave labor. Engines for Nazi night fighters and early jets had been tested in the two giant brick hangars beside the runway where today fluorescent-lit cubicles filled with anxious officers of the NATO armies gathered around maps and field phones connected to tactical operations centers hidden under camouflage nets in woodlands and marshes throughout north central Germany, and to airfields from Spain to Norway, to supply depots and mobile soil analysts and commanders from Frankfurt to Brussels. Such dark history all around, such potential for an equally dark future in the scenarios being played out here today, yet what gnawed at Spenser was something dark inside himself. He couldn't think of a thing to say.

The old British Sergeants' Club occupied a floor high in the flight tower, another brick and concrete monolith built to last a thousand years. The club had the down-at-the-heels feel of an abandoned roadhouse, which in a sense it was. Gilded trophies and punch bowls on the shelves had lost their luster, and water stains marked the paneled walls like unfurled maps. Windows that once overlooked the Third Reich's top secret aircraft framed a grassy field lined with row after row of sky blue portapotties awaiting distribution throughout the maneuver area. A Turkish tyrant and his teenaged sons had converted the club into a cafe of sorts.

By the time they were settled at a table in the empty dining room an eerie silence had come over them. A sallow young fellow took their order and went back to the shouting match in the kitchen. In a corner of his mind that had not completely frozen Spenser tried to piece together a soil science response to her question. It would be a calm and chatty disquisition about sampling stations, saturation levels, precipitation predictions and so on, but instead he heard himself say, "I have to tell you something." He hesitated. Was he really going through with this? "I think of you all the time."

There were things he had wondered for years. So many questions. His curiosity, he realized now, gazing at her while she seemed transfixed by the smelly tin ashtray in the middle of the table, was pitiful. How many children? Who was her husband? What did he do?

She heard him out and spoke carefully, as though giving directions to a stranger. A daughter sixteen, a son eleven. Her husband's name was Paul. He produced self-duplicating forms for shipping companies and the like.

"We seem to run into each other so often," Spenser said. "So many accidental encounters. I've wondered... It must mean something." His fingers fumbled with a paper napkin. "Doesn't it to you? Mean something, I mean."

Her composure was crumbling. Her words came in a rush. In grade school there had been a foreigner who could not speak the language, always alone, and then one day he was gone. "I try to draw you out, that's all. For me it's nice to see you smile. We should be friends, don't you think? I am so sorry."

He had foreseen this outcome, even rehearsed for it. He'd have everything under control. Much as he may have misjudged her, he would remain calm and civil. She would think he handled it with class.

She was shoving her arms into her raincoat and saying something about the newspapers and her deadline. The keys were in her hand. "Come along," she said, "or you'll be soaked."

He told her to go ahead. He'd be fine. She was gone before the coffee arrived.

Back at the gasthaus he stripped off his sodden jacket and jeans, tossed down a couple Excedrin, tuned to BBC and walked in circles. He was tempted to push the dresser against the door. He kept telling himself that people did stupid things all the time. What could they do, arrest him? All these years on alert, facing east. Our eyes on the Evil

Empire. What a fucking joke. What a fucking idiot. He packed up and waited until dark, then hauled his duffel to the car. He'd be gone at first light.

He was lying in bed fully dressed when there was a knock on the door. He followed the woman downstairs to the desk phone. "Wolfe here. The press corps is bailing out. They say the war's about to be called off. The farmers are bitching about the rain and their fields getting torn up. Aren't you supposed to be on top of this shit?"

"I'm not your man anymore. Talk to the colonel. Tell her you need a new escort."

"Bullshit. She said you belong to us for the duration."

"Can't help you. Sorry." He hung up.

A few minutes later the woman was back at his door. A certain Colonel Krueger very much wanted to talk to him. "I'll call her back," he told the woman.

At first he made good time, speeding past wooded windbreaks that loomed out of the mist between alternating fields of marsh grass and pink heather. Then came cultivated flatlands – sugar beets and potatoes – flat as Nebraska. Tank country. If ever the flag went up, this was the designated killing ground, Ground Zero for armored Armageddon. He drove with the desperation of an escapee. He aimed to beat the crowd out of the maneuver area to the autobahn where he could floor the pedal all the way to Stuttgart. But more and more both sides of the road were becoming lined with tracked vehicles – great muddy Leopards, Challengers and Abrams tanks interspersed with personnel carriers and fuel trucks and flatbed haulers, the very monsters responsible for the damage to the fields. The bright trickle of civilian traffic was grinding to a halt in a canyon of stalled armor and greasy exhaust. To Spenser it felt like a trap.

A federal policeman in blaze orange waved the bus in front of him onto a side road. Spenser flashed his press credentials and followed. The bus groaned and lurched along a gravel trail and through an opening in the trees, leading him to an incredible scene, a riverbank crowded with soldiers and a mobile bridge hanging half-unfolded over the water. The bus parked and out came Peter Eversol of Independent Television News in a bulky turtleneck. Next camp Maynard Bostwick, foppish as ever in a sheepskin bomber jacket and flaming red scarf. Spenser realized with horror that he had fallen in behind the British press tour. He had arrived at what was supposed to be the grand fucking finale of the exercise, a combined mobile-amphibious assault by Blue forces against an Orange bridgehead. Shades of *A Bridge Too Far*.

As the British press lined up for watercress sandwiches or some such nonsense and a regimental band in scarlet tunics played the theme from *Ghostbusters*, Spenser got out of his car and wandered off leaving the door open and the motor idling. There had to be a way out. He could not be stuck here. It was like sinking in quicksand. He absolutely could not stand another minute with these people.

Brian McNair's jolly voice rang out from the crowd. "Aha! Johnny, at last! Come get your oaf out of the erector set, will you? He jumped the queue, just like old times."

McNair pointed to a familiar figure towering over the crowd in the basket of a cherry-picker. A face full of hair and a chest full of cameras. It was Stone. Standing belligerently beside the truck, hands on hips, was his furry accomplice Wolfe, and confronting him was an angry Japanese camera crew in green vests and baseball hats.

Suddenly Wanda Kreuger was in Spenser's face, spit-shined and razor-sharp in her starched camos. Even lost in helmet shadow her eyes blazed. She clapped her hands in front of his nose. "Deal with your damn people!" she commanded.

He ran. The band blurred past, and soon he was deep into the woods, plunging through a boggy gruel of leaves and muck, spattered by low hanging branches. He wasn't in shape for this, but he churned onward, drenched to his crotch. Ahead was the payoff – a convoy of army trucks grinding along a muddy track. He jogged alongside the last truck waving a pocket notebook like a man on a mission. Hands appeared over the tailgate and in no time he was tumbled aboard, sprawling among duffel bags and knapsacks. Smelly soldiers crowded the benches on both sides, M-16s clutched between their knees just like twenty-plus years ago and halfway around the world.

He couldn't believe his luck. They were dropped off at the redeployment area, the first stop for units heading back to the States. All he had to do was weasel his way onto a flight manifest, and this nightmare would be over. He had sold his soul for a cubicle and a pension, making a fool of himself in the bargain. He was desperate to leave Europe behind with all its humiliations and dead ends.

The place was like gold rush days in the Yukon, all mud and canvas and improvisation in the middle of a wind-swept plain. One tent was like *Gone with the Wind*, the Confederate wounded in Atlanta, a sea of cots and spilled open sleeping bags and sprawled bodies as far as the eye could see. The soundtrack was coughing. Everyone hacked and snorted. The next tent was all GI souvenirs – Elvis on black velvet, Conan the Barbarian, bloodhounds dressed like Holmes and Watson. One booth was full of cowboy boots, another with black satin 'Served My Time in Hell' jackets. Nearby, soldiers lazed at picnic tables eating hot dogs and popcorn. Soldiers meant opportunity, and Spenser approached a chopper crew in coveralls: "How you doing? I'm John Spenser, *Time* magazine. I've got to get my photos back to the States a-s-a-p and I'm looking for a lift." But they weren't heading back to the States, just happened to be stationed nearby. Okay, no big deal. There was plenty of opportunity around here. He attached himself to a plump major with a clipboard in one hand, a bullhorn in the other, and a liter bottle of Coke under his arm. "Just substitute me for one of your stay-behinds," he begged. "A guy in the hospital, that sort of thing. I got a deadline to meet." The major kept glancing at the clipboard. Spenser wondered if he was deaf.

In the next tent he held an empty beer mug in a death grip and tried to talk an ancient sergeant first class into sneaking him aboard the plane with him and his troops. What a story that would make! He had to speak up to make himself heard, but the guy didn't blink. Like the grunts around him who smelled of mud and fuel and farts, he had apparently just peeled off a chemical suit, and his camo fatigues had a crinkled, just-born look. The man kept spooning goulash into his mouth, an ancient turtle poaching in the sun. But then his scaly eyes flicked open, and with his thumb he gestured at Spenser.

Two MPs were working their way through the crowd. Spenser noted their cheap plastic Sam Browne belts and holsters – unchanged since his years on active duty. You would think a nation that can target every village in the world for annihilation could come up with a classier outfit for its military police. Like, say, the understated uniform of the German cop waiting by the tent flap, his pistol a discreet bulge under his pale green tunic. As the MPs approached, Spenser was thinking: they have a way with uniforms, those fucking krauts.

1989

———

JACK HAGAN CAME AWAKE PAINFULLY AFTER A night of too little sleep, too many cigarettes and a good start on a bottle of Scotch. He couldn't get Ernie Cornish off his mind. The Ernie Cornish he knew, or thought he knew, had seemed eternal. Solid as a rock. It was heartbreaking to come across this decrepit version. Even worse, the more he had tried to be a comfort, the more he upset the old guy. Jesus. Welcome to senility. If it could happen to a guy like Ernie Cornish, what hope was there for anyone? You live well, you're at peace with the world, you think you're ready to fade away gracefully and suddenly you're lost in a nightmare.

His big adventure was beginning to feel like a big mistake. A shower and fresh clothes helped. He lingered over breakfast. That helped too. Hell, he'd already come all this way. It would be ridiculous to flee home just because he'd had a disappointment or two. He'd hate himself before he even got there. What did he have to lose by finishing what he came for? One thought led to another. If a man sets out to come to terms with his son, he might as well try to get straight with the kid's mother too. Or at least make the effort.

This was certainly not a part of the plan when they had set out from Melbourne. Honora was to be his guarantee of civility and, with any luck, a quick, uncomplicated trip. He had been banking that young Spenser wouldn't dare open old wounds under the glare of her watery eyes. "Johnny, I'd love for you to meet your stepmom," he'd say with a wink and a smile. Together he and Honora would stuff the boy with good food and plenty to drink, and they would fill the evening with tales of life Down Under. There would be a note of sadness too, and regret, and for young Spenser, perhaps, a sense of unfinished business. But by her presence alone Honora would have kept things civil. They would make a clean getaway. So lovely to catch up with you, Johnny. Hello to your sweet mother.

But without Honora he was defenseless before both young John and his mother, so he might as well face the music. Drumlin, his old hometown and site of his first love and lasting shame was a short hop away. He'd meet her face to face if she let him, and he would fess up and roll with the punches.

In his day, the outlying districts had been bad-boy country – dirt roads, farms, isolation. Guys drove out here to settle scores or to live dangerously with a girl and a bottle of booze. Today he barely recognized the place. It was all vinyl-sided houses and lollipop colored playgrounds.

He followed the river through a shady neighborhood of grand houses and grand oak trees that had grown old together. A few blocks further along, at what used to be the edge of town, he went by the old armory where he and fellow would-be soldiers drilled and played basketball in the years before the big call-up. The parking lot had been expanded and was filled with sanitation trucks and city snow plows. A few minutes later he passed his high school. Old Main, darkened from age, had grown wings of bright red brick. During the lunch hour he and his pals used to take over the yard near the front entry, and some of the bolder girls breached protocol by mingling with them and stealing puffs from their cigarettes. Now that yard was a sedate park with benches and tables populated by old-timers on walkers and four-point canes.

Things had changed, yet the quiet midday feel of the place had not. It stirred something in him as he knew it would, sucker that he was. And in turn, his sense of foreboding drained away. In its place was curiosity. He actually looked forward to being with her. He imagined a table set with coffee and donuts. Sure, they'd be all nerves, but at least some of the old warmth was bound to break through, thawing them out for a frank, and with luck, forgiving heart-to-heart. A misty-eyed high came over him, part sorrow at what might have been, part nostalgia for what once was. But first she'd have to let him into her life one last time. Over forty years ago he had tried only to end up in jail.

Back then the Spensers lived on the tony east side, so that's where he would start. Her father had been a big shot at the diesel engine plant, and most of the houses bordering East Broadway had been built with factory money, but the street had since lost its grand canopy of elms, and some of the places had taken on the shabby appearance of student rentals.

The name was still on the mailbox. He headed up the gravel drive towards the familiar ivy-draped heap of brick and timber. In high school he had become a regular visitor, but he never got over feeling like a trespasser on this side of town. He parked by the back porch, got out and gazed up at her window. It was an old ritual.

Her family had always favored the back door because it was close to the garage, but given the frostiness of their parting and long-term separation he thought it prudent to present himself at the front door. He took a short cut through the bushes. He was breathing hard. As he approached the entry his hand went to his cigarette pocket, but he knew better than to light up.

He pressed the bell. At least he was making the effort. He would make peace if she let him. If not, well, he tried.

He pressed the bell again. She wasn't a teenager anymore either. The word 'frail' came to mind. He would be patient.

It was a big house. Maybe she hadn't heard the bell.

He went down the flagstone steps and walked across the lawn to a window framed by thick tendrils of ivy. A magazine lay open on a coffee table but no one was in sight. The birdfeeders in the backyard were empty, the birdbath dry. Through the windows of the sun porch he saw wicker furniture and dead plants aligned on a book case. He walked around to the back porch and opened the screen door. When he tried to visit after the war there had been a shock of Indian corn hanging by the door and butter cookies cooling on the shelf. He had sent a letter telling her when he was coming, a big mistake. A little boy came to the door. How old was he – seven maybe? Six? The kid looked up. Hagan said, "Johnny!" This was his very own son, yet who was he really? A regular guy? A momma's boy? Did he play with other boys? Had he ever been on a two-wheeler? Or had she already turned him into a hothouse kid, ruining him for normal life? Maybe he was a hopeless bed-wetter.

He followed the boy through the hall and into the living room. "You know who I am, don't you? Let's get to know each other. You got a ball we can toss around?"

"Not in the house."

"How about cards? Ever played gin rummy?"

They settled uneasily on the couch, a cautious distance between them. No answer. Was he taking too much for granted? Clearly the boy was his own son, but at this moment he could be something else too – bait. Little Johnny. What was he thinking?

Hagan had always refused to be impressed by this house, the snooty old English effect with its exposed timbers and cedar shingles and all that crap. It was the money that impressed him. Any child support he coughed up was chump change to these people. It was revenge she was after. Pay up or else. He had come hoping to make peace. He and Honora and the baby were living in a trailer park outside Madison and getting by on GI bill money. He was trying to be a college student, but he kept getting threatening letters from a lawyer about support payments.

He'd been betting that if he talked to her face to face she might give up the fight, at least until he had some real money coming in. Now he wasn't so sure.

For the sake of anyone lurking upstairs he spoke up: "Johnny, I'd sure like to talk to your mom..."

Just then he heard another vehicle grinding up the driveway. He rushed to the window over the kitchen sink. It was a police car. Bait, indeed. He had walked into a trap.

So he remembered the little porch very well, and he knew that if she was in the kitchen she would hear him at the door. He knocked, waited, then knocked again.

Back outside he lit up. He was feeling very tired. Such adventures were for younger men. An old-timer should be smart enough to get the message and go away.

He didn't know what to do. Another time and in another frame of mind he might have gone all over town looking up some of the old gang. Back in the day they'd all been mighty tight right up to Melbourne and the reassignment that may have saved his life while also forever setting him apart in some irrevocable way. It wasn't like he'd been given a choice.

But the smell of autumn in Drumlin was in the air, bringing to mind that old excited-for-no-reason giddiness of his high school years. He refused to mope.

He drove downtown. On a stretch of River Street long known for its blue-collar taverns he watched a tiny Asian woman emerge from one of those doorways closely followed by a little girl pulling a wagon. Both wore pink flip-flops. Drooping over the edges of the wagon was the biggest bag of rice Hagan had ever seen. So long, Frank's Tap.

A block or so closer to the Five Points, which in his day had been the bustling heart of town, a familiar marquee came into view: The Park. It was the hotel where the moneyed crowd went to frolic in the old days, as his mother witnessed first-hand as a housekeeper there. One New Year's Eve she got him a job checking coats. It was an eye-opener. Church-going grown-ups carried on like teenagers. Booze, sweat, perfume, smoke, and very loud music. You knew they were going to end up getting laid or puking their guts out or both.

He parked at the corner by the old music store where grand pianos in the canopied windows had been East Main Street's touch of class. Now the canopies were gone, and bags of popcorn, handmade candles, and trays of fudge had replaced the pianos.

The Five Points was dead at this hour. Hard to believe how full the streets used to be on a Saturday night, the food smells and noise, the prowling cars, the steamed-up windows. Now, nothing. Still, here he was back on his old turf, all grown up and then some, with money in his pocket and time to spare.

Hagan's father had been a slave to his gas station, so Jack had learned to improvise. Hungry for meat? Then shoot it out of a tree or pull it from a hole in the ice. Want to make out? Then borrow a buddy's jalopy. The good life was playing second base for Drumlin's National Guard team and a beery cookout after. But now what had been impossible in the old days was just a charge card away. What the hell. On the spur of the moment he decided to make good on a long forgotten vow. He would sign himself into the Park and with any luck enlist some companionship for the night, just like the naughty rich used to do.

He went under the marquee and through the grand entrance, or so it had always seemed to him, into a lobby that reeked of steamed cauliflower. A line of ancient figures was gathering by the dining room entrance. Drawn faces turned to the newcomer, some gazing hopefully and then turning away.

This was not the Park Hotel of his wet dreams. A greeting in bright red letters hung over the lobby desk: WELCOME TO PARK MANOR!

1988

———

J OHN SPENSER FLEW HOME ON AN OLD C-141 belonging to the Air National Guard. It might have been one that he encountered decades ago at Ton Son Nhut airbase on his return from an upcountry assignment. Back then the silvery Starlifter had been the pride of the fleet, towering over all the lesser, snake-skinned transports like a phosphorescent glacier. This one was an old war horse sagging under coats of dull green paint. They were delayed first by worn tires, then engine problems. Over the decades its aluminum ribs had encircled tense paratroopers, shrouded howitzers, drums of fuel, frozen turkeys for the boys in the field, rice for the starving yellow man, swarms of mute tribesmen and their squalling animals, milky-eyed survivors of natural disasters in the Third World, body bags, and grey-faced wounded strapped on litters.

On this flight there was just Spenser and a group of reservist musicians on their way home from a tour of some kind, college kids and music teachers from out west.

The flight, the book in his lap, and even the new

position waiting for him back home he owed to his long-time section chief. Turns out he wasn't such a jerk after all. In deference to Spenser's shame and disgrace he had hauled his shaggy self to Spenser's apartment, parked his shades atop his curly head, and with a big wet sigh got down to business. From his briefcase he took a stack of computer printouts the size of a big city phone book and plopped it on the kitchen table. "There's not much going on in our line of work, but who knows? Guys like us, with our skill sets, we're chameleons. We can fit in anywhere."

When he was gone Spenser started flipping through pages. The tropics appealed. Guam needed an administrative assistant. American Samoa, a personnel records specialist. For Huachuca, Eglin Air Force Base, Panama City... He dozed, paced, downed tankards of water to compensate for the dry mouth his new pills left him with. It was after midnight when he was shocked out of his fog by a position half a day's drive from Drumlin and his aging mother. A museum was under development at Camp Palmer, a tribute to local boys who were reaching the end of the trail. They needed a curator. It sounded like a dream job. How many army divisions had fought in World War Two? There must have been dozens, many of them home state National Guard outfits. What would it take? A big plywood image of the shoulder patch, some old weapons in display cases, walls of photos and maps and newspaper clippings. Plus a soda machine and picnic tables outside under a tree – anything to make the old boys feel they haven't been forgotten. He could ride this job out to retirement. He wouldn't have to break a sweat.

So much for a life of vigilance at the free world's dangerous frontier. So much for returning home a mysterious stranger, a guy with stories he could never tell. Who was he kidding? At least this job had a down to earth appeal. Hell, presiding over an obscure museum devoted to a bunch of guys who really had sacrificed for their country could turn out to be the best thing he'd ever done.

The book was an early volume from the so-called 'Green Series', a many-volumed record of challenges faced by the US Army in World War Two – from converting sewing machine factories into machine gun producers to the free world, to turning millions of jalopy crazy kids into warriors. Spenser had seen the complete series lining shelves in post libraries and commanders' offices, the volumes identically bound in forest green with gold lettering.

Savage Jungle, Ruthless Foe: The Hard Lessons of The Ponga Campaign was an exhaustive examination of the army's first offensive against the Japanese, and for Spenser it was hard going. For one thing, the war in the Pacific had always seemed like a sideshow to him. True evil, the ultimate enemy, was Nazi Germany. He had grown up in a household fixated on the crusade in Europe. When news from Europe came over the radio the room went silent. Nothing else mattered but that solemn voice. The war was over there, far, far away, but it might have been going on just down the street so stricken were their faces around the supper table. But the other war, the one in the Pacific, never seemed so urgent. The settings had such travel-poster names, and the enemy looked like such crazy run-amoks, that it didn't seem quite real.

Savage Jungle was an eye-opener. An army of draftees had been assembled in hastily constructed camps across the country that still smelled of fresh-cut lumber and paint. The young men were as raw as their barracks. Meanwhile industry was being mobilized, gun powder factories were going up in remote places, automobile assembly lines turned into bomber plants. Those new Sad Sacks in khaki embarked on their training with one foot in the last war and the other, all too often, in the local drunk tank. Generals were afraid the kids wouldn't fight. Lesser officers were afraid they wouldn't obey, and nearby civilians were afraid to leave home for all the uniformed strangers staggering around town.

But another citizen army had been called to duty almost a year earlier, the eighteen infantry divisions of the National Guard. They were volunteers who already had some training in fundamentals, and they had the advantage of being organized outfits with a chain of command. Those eighteen divisions were supposed to be the country's first line of defense. They were to be fast-tracked through training and rushed overseas to hold the line while that great, motorized draftee army was being assembled and motivated and trained. Thus the soldiers of the so-called 'Bold Eagle' division watched the Golden Gate Bridge fade into oblivion just days after the fall of Bataan. Newspapers back home told of 'sealed orders' and 'black-hulled transports' zigzagging into the south Pacific.

In a matter of months the Japanese had shocked and crushed white defenders and their colonial counterparts from Singapore to Rabaul. Australians woke up to find the beast at their door, a door that was wide open because most of their army was in north Africa fighting Germans. Their coasts were virtually defenseless. Waves of prospectors, missionaries, plantation managers and government officials fled from New Guinea in overloaded bush planes. The government released a pamphlet entitled *If Invaders Come.*

Meanwhile Bold Eagle soldiers headed into war on luxury liners hastily converted to troop ships, window-shopping through shipboard PXs that still featured swank paraphernalia of the sort ladies might crave for nights of dining and dancing under a tropical moon. Following them to God knows where were schools of flying fish and radio bulletins of the latest from Corregidor.

No wonder the people of Adelaide took heart as those arriving Yanks marched through their streets. Little did they know that the marchers were rubber-legged and out of shape after being cooped up in trains and troop ships for months. Yet more travel was ahead, and after that they would need a period of training and conditioning and indoctrination into jungle warfare. Their theater commander, a living legend named MacArthur, had only recently arrived from the debacle in the Philippines. He was desperate to shake off the hunker-down mentality that gripped the continent and to strike back at the encroaching serpent. In Papua New Guinea, across the Coral Sea to the north, a thin line of Aussie troops up in the mists of the Owen Stanley Mountains had beaten back a Japanese attempt to take Port Moresby and thus lay claim to the whole island. The serpent retreated, his surviving soldiers exhausted and starving. MacArthur's intelligence officers were convinced that only a few hundred dead-enders were left defending a beachhead called Ponga Station on the north-east coast of the island. He wanted American soldiers to finish them off.

So why waste time immersing these newcomers into a program of jungle training when they could learn on the job? Thus the travel-weary Bold Eagle division became the first US Army outfit to go on the offensive against the Japanese and the first to flounder through uncharted jungle into well-laid traps.

The recent appointment of Major General Graham Chandler as commander of the Bold Eagles had lifted morale from top to bottom. Chandler was the real thing, a West Pointer, a former instructor at the Infantry School at Fort Benning, and a personal friend of the chief of staff of the army, General George Marshall. He was known for his cool head and savvy manner. He didn't shout; he explained. He did not look down on his National Guard subordinates but treated them as colleagues. Army friends thought of him as a scholar. Years ago Marshall had assigned him to conduct a critical study of the small unit tactics used by our army in the First World War. He seemed just the man to lead the raw young Bold Eagle soldiers into war.

General Chandler was at the airfield to wave off advance units – 'the tip of the tip of the spear', he called them – as they mounted C-47s for the flight to Port Moresby, the last remnant of civilized life on the island of New Guinea.

Four months later, in January 1943, the handful of Bold Eagle riflemen still on their feet wandered the beach at Ponga Station picking off Japanese soldiers who struggled through the surf to reach open sea. Most of the enemy had already been accounted for. They had been incinerated in bunkers or blasted out of trees, bayoneted in fetid aid stations, outflanked and overwhelmed in machine gun nests or they had starved to death at isolated outposts. Those who survived long enough to plunge into the sea were no luckier. They came sprawling back to shore by the dozen, a scum line of tangled limbs and bloated faces wreathed in seaweed.

Just about everything had gone wrong for the Americans along the way, but one thing was clear. The orange sun of the Japanese empire would never again fly over Ponga Station. The victors – by then a band of hollow-eyed invalids – were airlifted back to their tent city outside Brisbane to convalesce.

Spenser had a hard time with this story. Growing up, he'd heard of the Ponga campaign because fathers of high school friends had fought there, but that's all he knew. He couldn't find Papua on the map and had never bothered to look. Like every kid who'd learned about the war from Saturday afternoon double features, he took for granted that the Americans had kicked Jap ass there and everywhere else right up to V-J day. But the book in his lap was not a kick-ass story. The setting alone was a Stone-Age hell where tropical fevers and dread of the unknown were as disabling as the enemy and where your world shrank to as far as you could see through the smothering vegetation.

It was embarrassing to read about men his mother might have known in school shrinking from contact with the enemy.

The Ponga campaign had been the topic of rancorous debate ever since. The training exercise with live targets that MacArthur and his intelligence section predicted had become a slow-motion meat grinder, sidelining what was left of a whole division for nearly a year of rehabilitation. Initially denied its most devastating weapons, the artillery that was too unwieldy to transport over the mountains, the Bold Eagle had been handicapped from the start. One regiment was sent up into the mists of the Owen Stanley Mountains, headhunter country, along ancient trails that few white men had ever dared to traverse. Another was shipped around the coast in a collection of so-called luggers, wooden boats unfit for the open sea that had to hug the coast, and the other ferried over the mountains in a succession of airlifts.

By the time all the pieces were in place, soldiers were already delirious from malaria, dengue fever, and other wasting diseases. Battalions had been separated from their regiments in order to seek out the enemy along different routes, further splintering the division. More often than not the leading company stumbled down jungle paths single file into killing grounds where the enemy waited and watched from treetops and foxholes and bunkers so eerily indistinguishable from the surrounding foliage that GIs stumbled over or past them only to be shot in the back. The defenders they encountered were not dead-enders but veteran formations newly arrived in Papua. No wonder GIs panicked and got bogged down, some getting lost in the swamps and abandoning weapons in their rush to safety.

As he tramped over footpaths to forward positions deep in the jungle or at swamp's edge, General Chandler took in the bad news. It was clear that he faced not only a military crisis but a personal one as well. His boss over the mountains expected total victory right away. That wasn't going to happen. What matters most, General – your mission or your conscience? Your career or your decency? Something had to give.

Who to blame? MacArthur for grossly underestimating the challenges? Not likely. For officers of the regular army the easy scapegoat was this division of so-called 'citizen soldiers', heirs to the Minute Man tradition as they liked to fancy themselves, yet when put to the test, inept, undisciplined, poorly led and simply not up to the task. Paralysis in the face of the enemy; one bungled operation after another; cold feet up and down the chain of command.

So what would you do, Division Commander? Suppose your people are underequipped, out of shape, and undertrained. Your small unit leaders are mostly untested civilians with lackluster military backgrounds. Suppose delays, fevers and fear sap morale, and your first encounters with the enemy are disasters. Suppose you lack the firepower to crush him in his bunkers, and your green troops are bewildered and sick. Your mission is to destroy the enemy whatever the cost. What do you do?

Sunk into a sling seat belted to the fuselage, numbed

by the roar of the engines, Spenser was riveted. A disheartening tale in a repellant land had overcome his resistance. Never before had a story of dread, terror, and humiliation so possessed him. To clear his head he set the book aside and reached for copies of *The Stalker*, the newsletter of the division's veterans' organization. A dozen copies had showed up in his mailbox as he was about to leave Germany. They were densely printed, mimeographed affairs that might have been run off in the editor's basement. Decades ago it might have been a lively publication, but these days it consisted mostly of brief messages about connections made for one last time or regrettably missed. Wives announced the deaths of husbands, and vets urged that letters be sent to ailing buddies. A few simply sent a 'fond hello' or a 'big howdy' to distant comrades. Datelines ranged from Vermont to Texas to Australia.

These old guys were his bosses. They would want a museum that told the story as they had lived it, yet there was no avoiding the grim depiction of their outfit in the official history. It was hard to imagine a museum devoted to a humiliation.

Had anyone collected oral histories, or would that be his job too? Money would have to be raised, artifacts collected and catalogued. It was his baby. His section chief had depicted the job as a no-sweat glide to retirement: a remote setting, a disappearing generation, a minor story strung together on a few walls. He was not so sure anymore. What had he gotten himself into?

* * *

He paid the cabbie and took in the melancholy scene. Untended lawn, shrubs in disarray, windows disappearing under runaway ivy. It was about what he'd expected.

He hauled his duffel bag and suitcases onto the back porch and dug through his wallet for the long-buried key. In the hallway he called out: "Hello! It's me, home from the wars!" As expected, there was no welcoming reply. The kitchen table was stacked with unopened bills and bank statements. A Christmas cookie tin held pill containers. The refrigerator stood open, empty and unplugged. The faucet coughed out a splash of rusty water before running clean. Cupboard doors opened onto the same set of china, the same worn utensils, probably even the same tins of clove and cinnamon. The instant coffee smelled decent. He filled the kettle and turned on the stove.

Upstairs, three blazers in clear plastic bags were laid out on his mother's bed. Price tags dangled from the cuffs. Alongside were pairs of slacks and boxes of shoes. Clearly she had not given up her habit of assembling outfits as though in anticipation of a grand encounter and a new life, though in the past they had mostly ended up at Goodwill unworn.

The kettle called him back to the kitchen. He cleared a corner of the table and sat. For days he had been trying to make a list in his head, but it never quite came together, and the effort only added to his anxiety. So much to do, so little time. He tasted the coffee and dumped it into the sink.

Hours later he woke in a panic. He was curled on the living room sofa. The windows were dark. He grabbed his jacket and headed for the garage. The car was an Oldsmobile, a gaudy old lady in faded red. The engine sputtered and complained but soon ran smooth.

Not until he saw streetlights curling away into the distance did he lose the panicky feeling that he had fallen behind. Maple leaves drifted past the windshield. Empty streets were his sedative. The wind evoked the sound of Friday night football, but he knew from his mother's letters that the old stadium was long gone. The new one was in a suburb on the western edge of town well beyond hearing.

The Five Points, the center of night life in the old days with its steak houses, pizza joints and movie theaters, had turned as bleak and chilly as the vapor lights that now towered over them.

He parked across the street from the Park Manor. Women lounging in the lobby looked up when he came through the door. One reached out and caught his arm. It was Agnes Sydow, his many-chinned biology teacher. Come to think of it, she had been one of his mother's favorite teachers too. "So good you're here," she said. "She needs cheering up, poor girl. She doesn't even come down for meals anymore."

Landings were decorated with jigsaw puzzles lacquered and framed for posterity – a little girl in a sun bonnet tossing corn to chickens, a barefoot boy asleep beside a fishing rod. Nameplates on fourth-floor doors read like his mother's Christmas card list: Betty Webster, the pharmacist's widow; Rita Comstock, widow of his mother's lawyer...

At her door he hesitated, ashamed of his sense of dread. He knocked softly, then eased the door open.

She was sitting in the dark, gazing at the thermal hood on her supper tray. He knew immediately why she had abandoned the dining room. A long-festering annoyance had become a monster – a waitress with a sharp tongue or an icy glance from a table-mate. It could have been something as simple as the pattern of the wallpaper that had infiltrated her mind and mutated into something sinister. She was hiding out again.

"Take a look, Mom," he said. "Maybe you'll like it."

She looked up. Suddenly the old excitement was back. How she used to rush to the phone, the mailbox, and outside to meet a car heading up the driveway. Always such elation when the long-awaited arrived.

"Johnny! Why didn't you call? I've been waiting ever since I got your letter." It took her a moment to get to her feet. "But I don't eat," she said as they hugged. "I'm not hungry."

"Then let's go out. It's fall, Mom. The fresh air will give you an appetite."

"Maybe you could get my blue coat. And the blue shoes from the closet. Do you think I'll need a scarf?" She went into the bathroom, leaving the door open. She talked about the house. Her doctor told her it was just too much, and that's what caused her breakdown. "Too much responsibility for someone in my condition."

He burrowed into the wall of coats and sweaters jammed in her closet. The shelves behind were stacked with shoe boxes, old hat boxes, and six-packs of Ensure.

"Did you say it was chilly? Is this sweater warm enough do you think?" She flushed and came out and

sat on the edge of the bed. "I need help with the shoes."
He was rearranging a cardigan he'd knocked off a hanger.
Must you? he thought; I just got here. Already she was
reminding him where things stood. She was helpless. He
knew what would be next – water.

"Some water would be nice too. Just a little in a cup.
It's so dry in here."

As always the heat was cranked up high, and he was
sweating. "Do you have pills to take?"

"Pills? Do you think I should take my pills?"

"I'm just asking."

"I don't think so. Sometimes I lose them in the chair.
They found pills under the cushion. The nurse brings
them in a paper cup, but sometimes I drop them. Don't
forget my shoes."

* * *

She wanted a malted milk and a hamburger the old-
fashioned way with catsup and a pickle, so he took her to
the old Custard Cup only to discover that it was long gone,
and so too were the butcher shop and bakery that had
flanked it. In their places stood a sprawling new Wendy's.
The turn of the century walk-ups and lacy old elms lining
the rest of the block had given way to a Piggly-Wiggly and
a vapor-lit parking lot.

At their table near the salad bar she sat gazing at her
square hamburger and a frozen concoction called a Frosty.

"It's the best I could do," he explained. "It's what passes
for a malted nowadays."

"You know I don't think I can keep my room much longer. A woman wants it. I think they'll give it to her."

"Who told you that?"

"No one. I just know that she asked them about my room."

"That's her tough luck. You signed a contract, didn't you? It's your room."

"I know how it sounds. I just feel that they don't want me there. Like I'm intruding. I really do."

She was poking at her Frosty with a plastic spoon. It made a tapping sound but did not break the surface. A straw was out of the question. "It's awfully thick, Johnny."

"Let it sit. I'll get you some decaf."

"I don't want decaf."

"Tea?" he asked.

It was her luck to catch the eye of a Wendy's girl who was gliding a pan of taco meat into the steam table. Her face glowed from the heat. "Trouble, dear?" she said. The accent was familiar to Spenser. Mitteleuropa, he guessed. Her blazing red ponytail was deceptive. She was no teenager. She could have been his mother's age.

His mother said, "It seems to be frozen."

Such a dilemma. It was like old times. Something was wrong, something her son could not or would not fix, leaving her dependent on the kindness of a stranger.

"It *is* cold, dear," the Wendy's woman explained. "It's a Frosty, you know."

"You could heat it."

The woman was stymied. "Maybe in the warming oven, do you think?" she asked. "Soften it up a bit maybe?"

"You could try," his mother said. Her hamburger also posed a problem. She had lifted the top of the bun and discovered a slice of tomato. "If you get me a fork I can lift that thing off."

So much had changed and nothing had changed. He had gone off to war for God and country, had spent decades standing guard over Our Way of Life only to return to this. He had set out to find his manhood only to get caught up in the wrong war and spend his money years playing at foreign intrigue. He had not become a key player ever in anything – no notable achievements, no hard-won revelations about life and the world. Never did have much spunk, frankly. Hell, he couldn't even solve his mother's Frosty crisis.

They struggled to the car through blasts of wind-driven grit. Just as the engine roared to life, rain drummed on the roof. She wanted heat. Right away.

"Just turn in there," she said, pointing to the Piggly-Wiggly. "I need supplies."

He had purged his memory of that business. "Supplies?"

"You know."

He parked near the entrance and for a moment just sat there. Once again she was sending her little boy off to the store for 'supplies'. And once again, he would do as he was told.

"Ma, I wrote you about my new job, but you don't seem very interested. You had to know some of those guys in high school. Do you even remember the patch they wore?"

From her dark corner she said, "You know I don't remember things like that. You're the one with all the patches."

Roaming the aisles calmed him. It always helped to be in motion. He located the item in question, the same old brand now wrapped in plastic, and he tossed three packages into the cart. She still hadn't eaten so at the deli counter he got potato salad, seven-layer salad and slices of roasted turkey breast, enough for tonight and tomorrow.

He rushed through the rain with a bag hanging from each hand, then had to juggle them to free up his right hand to reach for the door. It was locked.

He thumped it with his knee. "Mom!" He leaned to the window but could barely make her out. "Unlock the door! Can you hear me?"

Waves of rain thundered across the roof. He splashed around to her side and thumped again. He could not see her eyes. Her face was in darkness but for a crescent of vapor-lit jaw.

"Ma! Look at me! I'm getting soaked!"

1989

JACK HAGAN'S THIRD-FLOOR ROOM OVERLOOKED AN
ocean of corn, wooded hills, and a sunset as melancholy
as a Sunday afternoon in winter. He was tired but he
couldn't sit still. His knees hurt but he couldn't stop
pacing. This place had an indoor pool but he hadn't brought
a swimming suit. It had a restaurant with a famous name
but he wasn't hungry. He was back at the motel halfway
between Drumlin and Camp Palmer, in farm country,
and he couldn't stop moving. He could not shake off his
embarrassment at barging into the Park pumped up on
X-rated fantasies. What a fool. And how sad! First the high
school and then the Park, long hotbeds of youthful passions
and – if you were lucky – deeds, both reduced to shelters for
people who'd outlived their so-called golden years.

A walk around the grounds and a healthy fruit salad
were no help. What to do? He hadn't jacked off for ages.
He could sprawl on that big bed and watch dirty movies,
but what a depressing way to end the day. He had come
halfway around the world to make amends to his son and

greet his old hero Ernie Cornish only to chicken out with his son and screw up with his hero. Even his hometown seemed to have turned its back on him. But no, he wasn't about to sink even lower by ending the day with his dick in his fist.

There was no hurry. That was the good news. He still had plenty of time to set things right with his son, or at least try. Now that poor befuddled Honora had shed that swollen hothouse of a body with its constant crises and endless medical appointments, she could wait in the car forever unencumbered by anxiety, impatience and other human frailties. Nothing could bother her anymore. He thought of looking through phonebooks for familiar names, but then what? He wouldn't call anyway.

As the sun went down the glow over the horizon seemed to intensify. It was a mystery. He called the desk and they told him the light came from a new discount mall just off the interstate. Hagan headed for the elevator.

The place was mobbed. It smelled wonderful – from fresh baked cinnamon rolls to come hither vapors drifting from Victoria's Secret. Moms and pops and kids on shoulders, mini-mobs of rowdy teenagers, old folks in the slow lane alongside shop windows; Hagan went with the flow past fall fashions, high-end kitchenware, blue jeans for skinny people and gym shoes for aging mall walkers.

Somehow he got spun out of the traffic flow and ended up in a domed, starkly bright arena of fast-food vendors. He scanned the place for something familiar. Burgers, ice cream oozing from steel teats, pizza by the slice, tacos – but nothing remotely sea-foody or curryish. A gin and tonic would have been nice too, as long as he was dreaming. At this late hour most of the tables under the dome were vacant, but sitting alone at one of them was a woebegone senior citizen who appeared to be taking a predatory interest in him. Hagan was irked. It was insulting to be sized up as an easy mark. Go after the old ladies, he thought. Bully the teenagers. Where was security when you needed them?

The pan-handler spoke: "Jack Hagan, you slippery bastard."

Hagan ran through his file of discards and came up with Leroy Abbott, class dipshit. Hagan's biggest disappointment as a trooper was when Ernie Cornish let Leroy into Machine Gun Troop. He didn't have to. It wasn't like they were desperate for recruits. Hell, they had a waiting list. Abbott showed up at his first drill with his stupid slide rule belted to his hip, just like in school. Hagan liked to believe that Machine Gun Troop stood apart from and over your run-of-the-mill outfit. With Abbott aboard he wasn't so sure anymore.

"Well shit, Leroy," he said, "you survived."

"Ha! Jack Hagan and his dancing fingers. Where you been hiding since you bailed out on us?"

Hagan pulled out a chair and sat. They did not shake hands. "Fuck you, Leroy. You know I had nothing to do with that."

"Sure, I know and I don't give a damn. You weren't there when the shit hit the fan, so you bailed on us. Nothing personal of course."

"You look terrible and you're all alone. Where's your tin cup?"

"I don't need any fucking tin cup. I'm doing just fine. What about you? You got a movie star tan, you dress like a country club lush, but you look like a lost little baby. Fishing for a rich widow?"

"Why, are you pimping for one? I've been to a few reunions through the years, Leroy, but never saw you. Voted out of the club? Dishonorable discharge? Too cheap to pay the dues?"

"Reunions. A bunch of weepy saps patting each other on the back and getting shitfaced together. Who needs that? A lot of guys have good reasons to not show up, including our old hero-except-when-it-counts, Ernie Cornish."

Jack flushed. Even coming from a useless creep like Abbott such talk was blasphemy. "Come on, Leroy, what could you possibly have against Ernie? He recruited you, brought you into the fold."

"What did I know at seventeen? Hell, I never even asked him, never thought I had a chance, but here he comes and *asks* me to join. He thought it would do me good, help me get along better with all you cool guys. It was like being blessed by the Pope. But when we started crawling through that fuckin' jungle it didn't seem such a blessing anymore."

"He couldn't help that. He was a good guy, and he's going through a hard time. I just saw him. He's a sad case in his old age."

Abbott grinned, displaying a rack of perfect teeth no doubt provided free of cost by the VA. "Yeah, well no wonder. He damn near got driven out of Drumlin. No tarring and feathering, but more of a whisper campaign. He come back to the classroom after the war, but it wasn't the same anymore. People were calling him the Pied Piper. It was like he'd suckered us young guys into his big deal horsy troop, but then look what happened to horsy troop. When the going got tough he was hiding behind a desk in Australia just like you. I know, I know. He had nothing to do with it, he was just following orders and all that, but you tell that to the parents of guys who didn't come back or came back messed up, and it don't sit well. Eventually he caught on and went off to someplace where no one heard of him."

So that was Ernie's fate – an outcast. That was his payoff for trying to help a bunch of raggedy-ass kids turn into men.

"You're still bitter after all these years, Leroy. I hear the vets club is doing good stuff, turning old Building One into a museum for one thing."

"What we went through you can't put in any museum. Not even close. You can't hang those smells on a wall, or the godawful dread and hate we felt. Maybe you can pin up some old dressings full 'a fossilized gore, but how do you display a cheating wife? There's no way to teach people what we went through.

"But I know your interest in that museum, and it's not what they hang on the walls. You were so sweet on Susie Spenser. In way over your head with a classy girl who obviously didn't have her head on straight. Knocked her up, as I recall. A generation or two later, guess who's running the museum. A guy named Spenser with an s not a c. Ain't that a stitch?"

Jack winced. The leper had turned nasty in old age. "Jesus, Leroy, we hardly ever exchanged a word back then. All of a sudden you're a guy with a grudge. What gives?"

"I'm nothing but grudges. Grudges are my meat and potatoes. Anger suits me just fine. The docs at the VA said I should keep talking – as if I needed encouragement. I never been one of those too-painful-to-talk-about-it types."

"Talk about what?"

"What you missed with your hundred words a minute fingers or whatever the hell. Fast hands, faint heart, I always say."

"Come on, I had nothing to do with being turned into a clerk. You go where they put you and do what they tell you. You know that."

"All I know is, you weren't there with the rest of us. There's those that went through it and those that don't have a clue. You're in the second category."

Abbott's fuse had been lit. He was launched: "You gotta hand it to the Jap. He is a cunning cocksucker. Draws you in like a spider. Lured us away from everything that made us stronger than him, over the Owen Stanleys and deep into that devil's asshole of a jungle. We got no artillery to speak of because MacArthur wouldn't ship it over the mountains. We got no tanks because the navy was too chickenshit to haul 'em around the coast. Half of us was already sick with malaria and tropical shits and fevers that don't even have names. Bit by bit we ditched most of our stuff – packs, blankets, and so on. We got nothing but rifles, grenades, a few automatic weapons and our own fat-headed ignorance. The genius with all the stars on his collar said it was just a clean-up job. Wipe out a few hundred sick Japs and get the hell out. Talk about loonies running the asylum.

"So here was me and Mel Burnette and Homer Crandall with the rest of the platoon strung out behind us. You're trudging single file along this muddy track with all this slimy shrubbery lickin' and droolin' all over you, poking you in the eye, grabbing at your ankles and stinking up the place. You can't hardly see your own feet much less where you're headed. The rest of the company was somewhere behind us, and the rest of the battalion was strung out way the hell and gone behind them. We liked to fool ourselves that we was the ones doing the creeping up and that we'd catch 'em with their pants down.

"Shoulda been obvious to anyone with a lick a' sense that this was their choke point, but fever-addled fools don't have any sense, so of course that's where they opened up on us. Homer was up front scouting. He went down like a wet towel. Fire came from everywhere and nowhere. I heard Homer shout for a medic. Some lieutenant come running up yelling, 'Follow me, Bold Eagles!' He disappeared down the trail and off the face of the earth. For all I know he ended up in a Jap cooking pot because before it was over they were eating their dead."

Hagan saw two women look on from a distance, one young, one not so young. Plastic bags with famous names hung from their hands.

"Three COs came and went in three days. Two wounded, one dead. You remember Lawrence Ripley. By then he was first sergeant and became CO by default. They shot him in the back when he crawled on top of a bunker without even realizing it. Jerry Kilbourn, the platoon sergeant, crawled up to look for him. We found him dead too.

"Patrols got sent out looking for ways to outflank the Jap, but they got lost or ambushed, and some guys, hell, they just camped out a ways and came back full of excuses. Even if you got by their skirmishers what you stumbled into on both sides of the swamp was a maze of bunkers. Roofs of cross-layered logs, walls of barrels filled with sand, the whole works covered with vines and shit so thick you didn't see it till you tripped over it. You don't break through defenses like that with rifles and machine guns. A few dead-enders, my ass.

"Maybe you read in the book about Jap foragers that got through the company perimeter one night. The way he wrote it, it was no big deal, a couple sentences about who done what to who and that's that. But if you was there that night it never stops being a big deal. What they stumbled into was our evacuation point, just a bunch of wounded waiting to get the hell out – including me. I'd caught a mortar fragment in the back. Didn't hurt much at first, but then I come down all stiff and fevery. By the time they had me back with the wounded I was going crazy from pain. They give me a shot, and I woke up in the dark to screaming and howling all around me. One of the screamers was on the other side of the coconut log I'd been set down by. Turns out he was getting a bayonet in the gut, and other guys were getting stabbed and stomped on and whatnot. The Jap was after food, tripping over guys, digging through packs, prying open cans of bully beef and wolfing it down. Fucking rodents were stuffing their guts while they were stabbing ours.

"That's what you missed, Jack, and that was just the beginning. Eventually we battered and burned our way up the coast of New Guinea and on into the Philippines, killing them in their holes, starving 'em out, whatever it took – another two years and more. Maybe you read about it in the book, but we was there, those that made it to the end."

The women looking on had cautiously approached the table, one on each side of the talker. "Now, Leroy," the older one said, "it's time to go home." She had read the situation. She had been here before, and she knew the rules. Handle with care. Persist, but gently. "We got what we came for, and it looks like you got yourself into a huff."

Abbott flashed Hagan an evil grin. "My second family," he said. "They didn't know what they was getting into either."

"Okay, Leroy, you just come along now," his wife cautioned. Wife and daughter had each seized an arm. "Up you go," the young woman said. "You got feeling back in your feet? Can you make it on your own? We need to get something in you soon as we get home."

"I'm good. I'm good," Leroy said, his eyes on Hagan. "Been a pleasure, Jack. You don't know how long I've dreamed of filling your fat head with all the shit you missed out on thanks to your talented fingers. You always were known as a guy who was good with his hands."

Little mouthy Leroy Abbott, the biggest jerk in high school, had turned into Leroy Abbott, combat infantryman and proud purple heart awardee. Propped between two stout women he grinned down at high school hotshot Jack Hagan, clerk-typist. "I get your point, Leroy," Hagan said.

1988

———

JOHN SPENSER'S NEW JOB HAD BEGUN TO HAUNT him. It had taken on a sour expression and an old man's voice. It was running out of patience. It suspected that he wasn't up to the challenge. Explain yourself, it demanded. So he had family obligations. So what? He had yet to even show his face at Camp Palmer, for Christ's sake.

Still he could not bring himself to break away from his mother and her dilemmas. The doctors had kept her in the hospital a second day for more tests. Then a third day. It wasn't as though she'd be abandoned. The staff would arrange transportation back to Park Manor. But what kind of son would run off at such a time? She would *feel* abandoned, and he'd feel like a rat.

He paced in her room, paced in the halls, and killed time at the lunch counter where, mid-morning on the second day, inspiration struck. There was a university library an hour away in Madison. University libraries carried all sorts of arcane material you wouldn't find anywhere else, certainly not in the Drumlin public library where his mother had spent decades at the circulation desk.

He told her he would be back before visiting hours were over.

The university library did not have what he was looking for, but the library at the state historical society across the mall did, and he spent the rest of the day cloistered at a little desk at the end of a row of book shelves piled to the ceiling with bound volumes. Occasionally a distant door wheezed open and there were footsteps, but mostly he was alone with row after row of obscure publications that had been waiting generations to be rediscovered.

From the official history he had learned that in the mid-1930s Colonel Graham Chandler had been editor of a magazine called *The Infantryman*. Here was a chance to discover Chandler in his own words – back when he was still a lieutenant colonel with no idea what his future held.

The Infantryman had been the means by which the skeletal, Depression-era army reached out to far flung officers rattling around in ghost-town training camps left over from the Great War or assigned to duty with the National Guard or Civilian Conservation Corps. It was a handsome publication on slick paper. Contributors included big names like Liddell Hart and Heinz Guderian who speculated on the nature of wars to come. There were features on recent developments in Europe with photographs of new tanks, anti-aircraft guns and paratroop formations, and there were penny-pinching recommendations for training the cash-strapped army at home: how to get a few more years out of hand-pulled machine gun carts on bicycle wheels, how to rig a penlight to a rifle barrel or a flashlight to a machine gun for marksmanship practice when ammo was hard to come by.

Spenser had only to page through a few issues to conclude that Chandler was more than just an editor. He had become the voice of the army's infantry school at Fort Benning. He was reaching out not only to the small, dispersed brotherhood of regular officers but to the larger citizen army of part-timers in the reserves and National Guard, especially to officers whose specialized training was otherwise confined to correspondence courses. Over and over he reminded them that they were today's Minute Men. When war came, they would be the first to take on the enemy, buying time for the great draftee army to follow.

Spenser was especially drawn to columns Chandler wrote under the heading 'Lessons Learned'. George Marshall, the commander of the infantry school at the time, had assigned Chandler to do a study of small unit engagements undertaken during the Allies' final offensive of the Great War in the summer and fall of 1918. The 'Lessons Learned' feature, spread over a half dozen issues of the magazine, was an extended account of his conclusions and recommendations.

Lesson number one was obvious: the butcher's bill had been excessive. Time and again American soldiers had paid too high a price for little or no gain. Inexperienced junior leaders, panicked senior commanders, inadequate planning and preparation: these had been the harbingers of lives wasted in attacks that were doomed from the beginning. *We would not ask fighting men to drive nails with their fists, yet we have routinely sent them up against machine guns and fixed defenses without adequate supporting fire. The infantry division has hammers for such work – tanks and artillery. The commander who has not learned how to incorporate them into the attack is a threat to his own soldiers.*

Of the three variables – time, equipment, and lives – it was better to save lives and take a while longer to accomplish the job. *Too often a commander pressed to act by distant, ill-informed superiors allowed impulse to overrule judgement and sent his fighting men to their deaths in a lost cause.*

This was terrific stuff but time was running short. Spenser hauled his big books to a copy machine and an hour later headed home. He was eager to spend more time with Chandler's thoughts about command responsibility, and he couldn't help but consider what Chandler didn't know when he wrote those columns. In a half dozen years, green troops under his command would slog into the mist and muck of northern Papua blind to the traps they were about to fall into – a vast killing zone of hidden bunkers and entrenchments. And from his veranda over the mountains, a five-star theater commander and matinee idol named MacArthur kept up the pressure: Keep going! Wipe them out! No excuses! Fire any unit commander who hesitates! It was the same 'Do something!' mentality that Chandler had urged readers to resist in his *Infantryman* editorials.

* * *

They said his mother had suffered a mini stroke, a so-called *transient ischemic attack*, and she was at risk of a big one. She was still confused. Her judgement was impaired. She was not ready to return to her private room but should be admitted directly to the manor's nursing care floor. Meds were prescribed, referrals made.

She agreed – until Spenser walked her to the manor's front desk and she told the woman in charge that the nursing unit was out of the question. She'd be fine in her room as long as meals were delivered and a nurse brought her pills. She was able to walk through the front door. She didn't need a wheelchair. They couldn't force her upstairs. There was a huddle – nurses, aides and an administrator. Okay, she would be monitored in her room for now.

The phone was ringing when John got home from car shopping the next day. A nurse told him his mother had eloped. A camera caught her walking out of the front door around supper time. This morning a custodian at her old library called to ask if they were missing a resident. He'd found her browsing books in a basement storage room. Apparently she had spent the night. She told him that she was fine and asked for coffee and a scrambled egg.

Not until Saturday morning was John able to head north. They had moved his mother upstairs to the nursing floor. For all her objections she seemed almost relieved, even acquiescing to an ankle bracelet. In saving her from herself the nurses had liberated him.

He drove a used Chevy pick-up, a major purchase for a guy accustomed to government transportation, but worth it if it helped him to fit in with the people he'd be working with. On the seat beside him were folders with the Chandler editorials – already heavily marked up with notes of his own. He was beginning to see the Ponga campaign from a very different perspective thanks to Chandler's 'Lessons Learned'.

A leaden sky, a blurry horizon of yellowing hills and miles of sun-dried corn. Early fall. He looked forward to being alone. He'd need time to acquaint himself with a legendary building and the empty space he was expected to fill with a fading fragment of history. That elusive intelligence agent of his imagination, the guy who disappeared over the border to better serve his country monitoring a hostile world, was still with him in spirit but no longer a model for his own life. He had fallen sadly short. So John, what have you been up to all these years? Been overseas. Can't talk about it. What a joke. But when your glory-seeking days are over you pick yourself up and face facts. Such was life. Happened all the time. He was lucky to be serving a bunch of deserving old-timers. The spotlight was on them. What mattered would be the story they left behind, not his sad tale.

Spenser passed his ID up to the MP at the main gate. "So you're the guy," the man said. "At long last." He came out of his shack unfolding a map and leaned to Spenser's window. "Bear with me."

There were two Camp Palmers, he explained, but joined at the hip. Separate locations, separate histories. The big one was New Camp, which was built in the early forties to train draftees for the war in Europe. It consisted of a little city filled with tight-packed barracks, mess halls and so on plus the big wilderness training area. Old Camp Palmer was a small reservation in a corner of that wilderness. Old Camp had been in operation for over a century. That's where National Guard soldiers had trained since the Indian wars, and that's where Spenser's museum was located. The Bold Eagle had been based there long before World War Two, and it had been mobilized and sent south for training when New Camp was still just a mass of blueprints.

Spenser was lost from the start. The guy's finger jumped all over the map. No big deal. He had time to wander, and soon he was bumping over railroad tracks and passing cream-colored warehouses on one side, cyclone fence topped with coils of razor wire on the other. He emerged into a sprawling complex of double-decker wooden barracks that went on as far as he could see. They were so-called 'temporary' barracks of World War Two vintage, each with its own coal bunker. The pattern repeated itself block after block, broken at intervals by mess halls and supply sheds on shaggy fields. Except for deer grazing in one of those fields the whole place seemed empty of life. Clearly this was not the stripped down outpost known as Old Camp.

In yet another field, sheltered under a cluster of pines, a sprawling officers' club appeared to be wasting away in the embrace of a sagging porch. Spenser continued along the broken road, dodging potholes. At long last he spotted a van bearing government plates. It was parked at a building identified as Recreation Hall 3. He pulled up beside it.

The entry led past latrines to the left, an empty library room to the right, and opened into a great space lit from second-story windows. Stuffed furniture that might have come from a north woods tourist lodge was scattered about. At the far end of the room a grand piano stood near a stone fireplace. What a classy off-hours hangout for soldiers and their guests, Spenser reflected, but on second thought he was struck by something else. Clear out the furniture and you would have a terrific dance floor.

It was entirely conceivable that once upon a time a desperate young woman dragged her sleepy little son up the circling staircase in the corner so that she could better survey the dance floor. If this was not that very place, then it was a twin. He remembered his face pressing between the spindles. How bewildered he had been by his mother's fascination with the hand-holding couple below.

Footsteps echoed through the hallway. A workman stooped under the weight of a tool belt on one shoulder, an extension cord coiled around the other. He managed a smile. "You must be lost," he told Spenser. "No one comes here on purpose anymore."

Ten minutes later he was back among the aging warehouses, then acres of abandoned mid-century personnel carriers, road graders, bulldozers and other cast-offs. He bounded over railroad tracks again. In the deep gloom off to the left sprawled the bogs and piney hills of the vast maneuver area. At intervals dirt trails poked through the trees. They were marked by stenciled road signs: Fuel Point, Field Storage, Drop Zone...

He drove for miles through a wasteland of sand and stone before the woods closed in again and the air turned cool and sweet. Then, finally, a grassy basin opened up ahead, a sort of secret valley, bounded on one side by densely wooded hills and on the other by sandstone bluffs crowned with a sentry line of wind-scoured pines.

Far off on the grassy floor of the basin, three single-story brick buildings were arrayed in a semi-circle around an old howitzer and a flag pole. Up the nearby hillside, shaded by ancient oaks and overlooking the buildings, stood a dark-stained lodge made of logs with overhanging roof and wrap-around porch. This was the place.

He passed areas of the bluff that had been pitted by generations of rifle fire, the tall grass covering former firing lanes where a century ago sharpshooters in blue had wrapped themselves around long-barreled rifles and squinted through elevated sights, imagining Apaches at three hundred yards. Later, Depression-era high school kids bruised their shoulders squeezing off rounds from Great War-era Springfields, just like real soldiers.

He veered onto a dirt lane heading uphill and parked in front of the lodge's shady porch.

He mounted the wooden steps, and as he reached for the door it was opened from within. "You must be Mr Spenser!" the woman said. "I'm Louise, one of the volunteers. We thought someone should be here to show you around, so that's me. I hope you don't mind."

He hadn't expected this. He'd been looking forward to discovering the place on his own. "I'm afraid I got lost. I hope you haven't been waiting long."

"Not at all. I had time to scrub the bathroom. I figured you ought to have a clean bathroom at least." She pulled a scarf from her head, wiped her nose with it and stuffed it into a pocket of her jeans. "You can guess what this room was. The floor is pretty well soaked with beer."

A plastic Hamm's beer clock hung on the log wall between a pair of deer heads. Toy Sabre jets and Phantoms hung over a long bar with a fleshy shoulder of red leatherette. There was an earthy stink of bar-room excesses from ages past. A smoky mold of some kind was eating away the surface of the mirror behind the bar.

"Looks like an officers' club fallen on hard times," Spenser ventured.

"That's what it was in the end, the Air Guard's officers' club, but they say the building has been so many things through the ages – headquarters for the state militia in the old days, a dormitory, a lock-up and a storehouse, you name it. Of course everyone wants to meet you. They've been waiting so long to finally have a real professional take charge. It's been a long slog getting organized."

Spenser was trying to envision display cases spaced along the walls. "Everyone?" he said. It was a shock yet so obvious. This job came with social obligations. People had expectations.

"You know, the vets and the auxiliary. We help with the fundraising and so on. The fellas feel like their story got buried for so long, you know, so now the idea of finally putting it up for all to see has got people excited."

"I suppose," he murmured, but he didn't want to think about that now. What he needed was time and privacy. "What about you? You sound like you might be sort of a newcomer too."

That was very true, Louise told him. Her brother had

been one of the first to fall in the Ponga campaign, but she only learned about the auxiliary from a newspaper article. Late in the war and for years thereafter, friends in his rifle company trickled home one or two at a time, but none ever showed up at the door to say a few words. She kept running into them around town, but all she ever got was a shy hello, as though they didn't know how to talk about her brother's death in battle or didn't want to.

The next room was twice the size of the bar room and twice as dark. There was a smell of clothes long stored in airless places. In one corner stood a waist-high display case that might have come from a jewelry store. It was lit up from within. John peered down at a standard army headshot of a distinguished looking fellow with pale eyes – Major General Graham Chandler, at last. Alongside were curling five by sevens of Chandler surrounded by young, eager-beaver types clutching tommy guns and rifles, no doubt members of his personal staff thrilled to be photographed alongside the man they looked up to. On another shelf were copies of *Yank* magazine and an Australian publication called *Radio Call – South Australia's Radio Weekly.* The cover photo featured Bold Eagle musicians in classic Hollywood poses: 'US Army Swing Band in Action'.

From a water-stained carton of pamphlets John picked out a program from an early Bold Eagle reunion. A stack of steel helmets was on the floor. Dress uniforms hung from a rack. A pair of mannequins with chipped cheekbones and missing noses sprawled on the floor like bomb victims.

"So this is what we got so far," Louise said. "People

get to rummaging in the attic and this is what they find. Widows pass it on to their local vets' club, the club passes it on to the museum committee, and here it is, gathering dust. I don't think anyone knows exactly what we got, but there's a lot of it. And it keeps coming."

The last room was lit by a bank of fluorescent lights. Metal shelves lining the walls were stuffed with cardboard cartons, gas masks, brown cavalry boots, stacks of scrapbooks, a reptilian tangle of web gear hooked to dangling pouches and packs. Old sun helmets and all variety of obsolete headgear were scattered about willy-nilly.

A gun vault stood in a corner. Jack eased open the heavy door. The weapons looked like artifacts dredged from an Iron Age swamp. One he recognized as an M-1 rifle, the GIs' standard infantry weapon, but there were green stains on the barrel and the stock had been blackened somehow. Alongside it was a nasty looking short-barreled shotgun known as a 'trench sweeper'. The only other long gun was a spindly fencepost of a rifle, a Japanese bolt action also coated in black crud. On the floor of the vault, stuffed in a beat-up leather shoulder holster, was a government automatic identical to the one Spenser had carried in Vietnam. The last item might have been the spine of an animal, but the woman said the vets believed it was from a Japanese machine gun. The vault gave off an earthy, personal scent like the breath of a sick child.

Finally she led him through a door on the opposite side of the building. "And this is your kitchen, office, bedroom and whatnot all in one. It's the only place with a heater, and believe me, you'll need it soon enough." Grease blossomed on the ceiling like underwater flora. There were gaping holes and hanging conduit where a grill and deep fryer had been. A sink, a desk, a phone, an old Kelvinator refrigerator and a hotplate were all that remained, aside from a disassembled GI bunk stacked against the wall behind the door. The saving grace was a window overlooking the barracks and grassy basin.

"That's it, pretty much," she said, hefting a tote bag from the desk. "So I'll leave you to it. You let me know if you need helpers. I want to be part of this project because of my brother. I don't want to be left out this time." She handed him a key.

"I'll let you know," he said. He had already forgotten her name.

Alone at last, Spenser roamed the building, inhaling the smells of hard partying, old clothes, and smoke – his new domain. It was his to bring back to life one last time, from the creepy bar-room mirror to the sooty rafters. After generations of repurposing and reconfiguring and upgrading, old Building One was back to where it began, empty and waiting. This was his last chance to make something of his life, and he conjured a vision of something more substantial than a collection of dead things, something transcendent. Sure, there would have to be plenty of old pictures and maps and odds and ends. But there would be a message as well. Reputations would be restored. Long-buried history would be brought to life. He had taken the job as a safe hideaway in which to count down to retirement, but pacing one room after another he wondered if he had finally stumbled upon the mission he had been intended for all along.

1989

———

JACK HAGAN HAD ENOUGH. HONORA'S DEATH, THE botched visit to his old hero Ernie Cornish, a cold shoulder from his hometown, and a public humiliation inflicted by a nobody named Leroy Abbott – he got the message, and he was bailing out. This trip had been a mistake from the beginning, an impulse born out of a daydream. Young John Spenser could get along fine without him. He'd been back 'home', as he used to think of the place, only a few days, but it already felt like too long. He got up slowly and late, nursing the headache he deserved and fiercely determined to get back to O'Hare by the end of the day. Only after the rental car was off his hands and flights were booked through to Melbourne would he dare settle his bones down for a big bloody steak and an anesthetizing round of martinis.

But first, shamed by Honora and her dread of customs people pawing through their dirty clothes, he bundled his grubby stuff and headed to the laundry. By the time he got to the cafe he was winded, craving a smoke, and too late for breakfast. The waitress sat him at a table that was already occupied. The others were being prepared for lunch, she told him. He ordered coffee and a piece of yesterday's apple pie.

His reluctant companion was a woman about the age of his daughters. She acknowledged him with a half-smile but refused eye contact. The way she huddled with her mug made him feel like he was butting in on something personal. He liked coffee too, but she was overdoing it. He had gone to sleep bitter and lonely. He woke up cranky. Her evasiveness was a provocation. He sized her up like he and his buddies used to do it in the old days, coldly. She'd been around. Probably had her share of rowdy times, though today was obviously not one of them. More likely it was the morning after. That was fine. He had a taste for worn-out babes. She wasn't bad at all.

"Travelling far?" he asked.

"Mm," she said. "You?"

"I will be. I'm heading back to Australia where I belong." He was loud on purpose – the ugly Aussie. He was a recent widower on his last trip home. He had been thwarted at every turn. Nobody seemed to give a damn. "I was trying to meet up with my son, but it didn't work out."

She eyed him cautiously. "That's too bad."

His wounded pride gave way to curiosity. "Where are you headed?" He turned to his coffee and pie.

"So you're from Australia," she said, again evading his question.

"Not originally, but yeah, since the war."

"I don't think I ever met anyone from Australia."

"Wonderful place. Beautiful. Like around here but with kangaroos. And friendly people." He wondered if she knew anything about the war in the Pacific. Would she listen or would it put her to sleep? Aware of his own face heating up, he was struck by how pale hers was. She was squinting as though even the dim lights of this shadowy room hurt her eyes. "I grew up in Drumlin. We were sent to Australia early in the war when the Japanese were a threat there."

An awkward interval passed. "So you'd be heading to O'Hare, right? Heading south?"

"I am."

"Would you consider giving a stranger a lift? I'm trying to get to New Franklin."

"Never heard of it."

"It's just off the interstate. Won't add more than twenty minutes to your trip."

Hagan gazed at her. It didn't add up: alone and sucking coffee in a motel far from home, no car and apparently no money.

"I'd have a ride eventually," she explained, "but I'd sure like to get home sooner."

Rhymes with nooner, he reflected. "I guess that would be alright." He considered the possibilities. "Of course I'll give you a lift. It would be nice to have your company." He was far from home. He would be gone from her life within hours. He had plenty of cash, if that was a factor. Good Christ, was he going to get laid? How long had it been? Was he being a fool or a jerk or both, and did it matter?

She was a nice-looking woman. She would have a nice

warm belly and a nice fleshy scent. She was a generation younger than he was and so, by definition, young. To clutch her to him would bring tears of gratitude and relief. Yet she was so pale and crumpled in on herself. Was she, in some way, 'not well'?

"So," he said. "I'd like to get underway. I have to check out. How about you?"

"I'm ready any time."

"No bags?"

"No bags."

Outside, he plucked a pack of cigarettes from his pocket and extended it to her, assuming that with her familiar cough and stained fingers she'd be desperate too. She waved it away.

He led her to the car. "So you're quitting. Good for you."

It was an overcast day heavy with mist. She walked with her head down, her jacket gathered tight around her.

"Am I right?"

She thought about it. "Trying to. I sure don't feel like one now."

He put his suitcase in the trunk and opened the passenger door for her. She hesitated. "A gift for a lady?" she said.

"Oops, my mistake." He snatched Honora's container and hurried back to the trunk, then got behind the wheel exhaling mightily. He lit his cigarette and took a deep drag. "No, no, not a gift, I'm afraid," he said, exhaling smoke. Then, "Oops, another mistake." With the engine running he got out of the car, sucked heavily on the cigarette a few more times and crushed it underfoot. "I won't smoke in the car. Might have to pull over from time to time though."

"It's all the same to me. Whatever you want."

He accelerated off the ramp onto the empty freeway. "I'm Jack Hagan, by the way."

"I'm Vivian."

"Ah, lovely name. Vivian. Old-fashioned, if you don't mind me saying."

"My mother loved *Gone with the Wind*."

"Was she a southern girl?"

"No. She grew up on a farm near New Franklin."

"And your father?"

"He was from the farm across the road. High school sweethearts. Four H club and all that. An old story."

"Nothing wrong with that old story."

"They were teenagers when I was born."

"Ah well. That happens, doesn't it?"

The fields had been recently harvested, stalks and all. Nothing but miles and miles of corn stubble in endless rows like lines on a contour map. From time to time he turned on the wipers.

"You know, Vivian, I must confess that more than once in my long life I've come awake with a very bad headache. I have a bottle of Scotch in my suitcase. Think of it as medicinal. A sip or two might ease you into a brighter day so to speak. Up to you, of course. I've got to stop soon anyway. Just so you know."

After pulling into the next rest stop he dug the half-filled bottle from his suitcase and put it in the footwell in back with a collapsible metal cup. Vivian looked on and then they went off to the rest rooms. After an unproductive minute or two standing at a urinal Hagan walked out back where the trucks were parked and lit up. Finished with his cigarette, he returned to the men's room and stood at another urinal before finally giving up.

When he got back to the car he discovered that Vivian had moved to the back seat. He turned the key and checked the rear-view mirror. She was smiling at him. "On second thought," she said, "maybe I would like a cigarette."

She had crammed herself into a corner. There seemed to be more color in her face though it was hard to be sure in the shadows.

"So when you get home, Vivian, will you be alone?"

"Why do you ask?"

"Oh, out of concern, I guess."

"Concern I might pass out?"

They were back on the interstate, and with increased speed the windshield was soon spattered. He flicked on the wipers. "I don't know about that, but you have seemed a little under the weather."

"I'd be home. What's to worry about?"

"Well, probably nothing, but..."

"Aren't you a merry old soul? And Cindy thought you looked like such a gentleman."

"Cindy?"

"The waitress."

"Ah, so you were in cahoots. A geezer totters into the dining room and the conspirators think, 'Old and feeble, a safe ride at last!'"

"We stayed up all night drinking coffee. This morning

they called her in for a double shift. She'd have taken me home later if she had to, but it would have been a long day for both of us."

He smiled back at her image in the mirror. "I see. So the gentleman obliges, and here you are in his car and suddenly he's not such a gentleman anymore. Vivian, please. I have expressed concern, that's all, and maybe some normal human feelings as well. Do I miss being physically close to a woman? Guilty as charged. There's no shame in that."

"That thing you put in the trunk. It isn't a gift for your wife, is it? It *is* your wife."

"Her ashes, yes."

"But here you are, you naughty man, already trying to get into another woman's pants."

"Fair enough, but wouldn't you feel good consoling an old man who travelled halfway around the world to the town where he was born and raised only to have one door after another slammed in his face?"

She exhaled smoke at the ceiling. "Aren't you the least bit ashamed?"

"Honora would understand, believe me."

"Honora! That's her name? Christ, and I thought Vivian was bad."

"She was a wonderful human being and quite the gal in her day. Her name was a perfect fit."

She said, "Tell me about Australia."

He welcomed the change of topic, but as always he could not talk about his adopted homeland without starting with the war years and what a big deal it had been for kids just out of high school to climb aboard ritzy ocean liners converted to troopships and to churn into the Pacific knowing that half a world away, in some jungle hell hole, the enemy was waiting.

The next road sign pointed west to New Franklin. The turn-off led to a weathered two-lane.

What a thrill to come ashore on the far side of the Pacific and be greeted by crowds of white English-speakers. They felt like heroes simply for showing up. Much as he wished for her sake that he could carry his story into the savage bloodletting of the Ponga campaign, he could not. As Leroy Abbott had mockingly reminded him last night, he'd been denied the privilege of going into battle for his country because there was a critical need for him in the typing pool. His good fortune then had become his eternal shame.

"So you had it easy," Vivian said.

"Such was my fate."

"While the others were fighting and dying, you were fucking a flower girl."

The wallflower was baring her teeth. "Aren't you the sassy one?" he said. "I married that girl. We had a long, happy life together. We had two wonderful daughters who are grown-up women with daughters and jobs and good lives of their own, and they love me in spite of my wandering ways."

"Huh. I've heard about men sleeping with their daughter's friends."

"Vivian, I refuse to be the harmless old fool you took me for."

"Still haven't tamed that silly old thing, a worn out stud like you."

Her head slid from view, and he heard a sound like crinkling cellophane. The air was already thick from cigarette smoke and damp clothes, but something sweet had been added to the mix. It brought to mind the warmed-up mashed bananas that his mother used to spoon into his mouth eons ago.

"Are you sick?" he said.

She coughed and spat. "You might say that," she choked.

"Vivian, for Christ's sake, don't you dare..." Dare what? Befoul my rental car? Shame me this way? Choke to death?

A pair of grand, sun-bleached old houses stood on a hillside just ahead. Facing them across the road was a stretch of storefronts. Hagan pulled in at the gas station and rushed around the car to her door. Vivian was crumpled on the floor. Her eyes were closed. "Get your face out of that stuff," he said. "Can you sit up?"

A heavyset woman in winter boots and a snowmobile suit emblazoned with 'New Franklin Co-op' patches marched up. Hagan was struck by her mournful eyes.

She poked her head in. "Come on, Vivian, sit up." She leaned over and heaved the limp woman onto the seat. "Hold her up," she told Hagan. "I have to make a call." She hurried to the office.

Hagan was confused. The word '*vile*' came to mind and with it a vision of Honora's piercing, flash-frozen glare. It was no joke this time. He *was* vile. And yet he didn't know the girl had a problem. Hadn't he meant well, or mostly well? How could he have known?

An old Honda pulled up. The driver was a young woman underdressed for the weather. A little girl was belted into the back seat. The woman rushed around to where Hagan was standing, brushing him aside. "Oh Mom, damn it all to hell, you got sick all over you."

Vivian's eyes were halfway open. She might have been attempting a smile.

The young woman turned on Hagan. "And you are?"

He tried to explain – table companions at the motel cafe, the request for a ride. If only he had known.

By then she had turned her back and was tending to her mother. "Cindy's her sponsor. She'd never let her come home like this. Mom was having a hard time, and Cindy was keeping her safe overnight. Now look. You bring her back like this." She shot a glance over her shoulder. "You did this, you creep."

The attendant said, "You have to get her to detox, Joanne."

Together the two women hauled Vivian to the Honda and strapped her into the back beside her granddaughter.

As the car roared off Hagan braced himself against the door frame, still sucking in the tainted evocation of mashed bananas. It might have been poison gas so wobbly had his knees become and so dark was the chill creeping over him. With fingertip and thumb he retrieved the nearly empty bottle and dropped it in a trash barrel beside the gas pump.

The co-op woman trudged past him wiping her hands on a rag. He looked to her eyes for some sort of acknowledgement. For a minute or two hadn't they been

Samaritans together, allies in a common cause? But she passed by without a glance, as though he was already history as far as she was concerned.

1988 – 1989

NIGHT TIME TESTED SPENSER'S RESOLVE. DOUBT returned. He lay in the dark wondering what he had gotten himself into in the middle of his life, in the middle of nowhere, alone in a ghost camp. Occasionally a squirrel scampered over the roof and occasionally an acorn landed like a spent bullet. So much was expected of him by a fading army of old men who remained, to him, just names on a mailing list. Such a strange place. Such an unlikely enterprise.

Daylight made all the difference. Then the guy who had day-dreamed the years away in Germany came to life full of can-do spirit and craving connection. Above all he yearned to reach out to those old men, and the best way to do it, he decided, was to get their stories on tape while there was still time.

And so one sunny afternoon in late October he sat in the screened-in porch of a big white farmhouse in hills north of the town of Harding, only a few miles from Old Camp Palmer, as Elda Whitney turned pages of a photo album while her husband, Robert, still in his overalls, squinted over fields of drying corn. "No one had money back then," she was saying. "No one went anywhere. If you saw a vehicle on the road it was probably a milk truck. That's why the Guard was such a big deal. It made the family feel attached to the world, what with the fellows wearing a famous insignia on their shoulders and the radio full of awful happenings overseas. Look here – the winter formal in 1937, all those young lawyers and farmers and whatnot dragging those silly swords around. But weren't we a handsome bunch? Remember, Bob, the venison and wild duck? All the ladies brought something."

The colonel spoke up: "Some 'expert' gave a talk about horse cavalry, how we'd always need it, tanks and airplanes being too fragile to stand the stress of modern warfare. He got drunk the next summer and impaled his horse on a picket fence."

When the division was called up a few years later Whitney was the only Battalion commander most of his soldiers had served under. He'd kept them together when Depression-era budgets had limited weekly drills for his four scattered rifle companies to chalk talks, weapons assembly and close-order drill in coal-fired armories and rented warehouses. He led them through the chaotic months of mobilization, a year of training and modernization in Louisiana and the sprawling mechanized war games through the summer of '41, and a year later into a jungle halfway around the world.

Spenser had so many questions. He pressed Whitney about the Ponga campaign and the ordeals they went through just getting to the front. What about the aggressive orders he felt pressured to follow even though he lacked information about enemy dispositions? What did he make of General Chandler and how he dealt with demands from MacArthur for success now, whatever the cost?

But the old colonel seemed reluctant, as though the whole nasty business was beyond the comprehension of a come-lately guy with a tape recorder – or simply too painful.

"Okay," Spenser said. "Let me jump ahead. MacArthur expected an easy walk-over. It didn't happen so heads had to roll, and suddenly you're on a C-47 flying back to Australia with all the other officers for whom the division had been like a family, all of you destined to spend the rest of the war at desk jobs far from the sound of guns. MacArthur's hand-picked regulars fly in to take over the division with MacArthur demanding victory right now. What was it like having to take the blame for a guy who was too vain to admit his own mistakes?"

Whitney was gazing sourly into the distance. Spenser knew he was poking an old wound. Was he poking too hard?

The colonel's hand rose in a grand, dismissive sweep. "MacArthur," he sneered. "I'd walk a million miles to piss on his grave."

Spenser drove off a happy man. At least he'd come away with one nugget. It was pure gold, and he had it on tape.

Cruising country roads through the shadows of early evening he felt a kinship with the lone wolf correspondents he had idolized in his youth. Like them he was pursuing an elusive story in obscure places. The vets were scattered in river towns and farm towns and old villages in shady valleys. He'd park, grab a sandwich and walk through the heart of town in the fading light to get a sense of the main street his next interview had marched through that cold October night before the trains swept them south, away from peacetime drill and summer camp rituals into a no-nonsense world of tight schedules, short tempers, swollen feet, and bewildering war games of the mechanized age.

On the road that fall he encountered trucks bearing the inscription BOLD EAGLE FREIGHT, a billboard outside of Mayville promoting BOLD EAGLE ROOFING, and a playground village in Elk County named BOLD EAGLE PARK, with weathered teeter-totters, swings, and monkey bars out of the age of wood and iron. The name endured, but what did it mean to those kids and their young parents, if anything?

On an Indian summer afternoon in Fair Oaks, a valley town tucked between hills spread with apple orchards and goat farms, he sat on a front porch with Oscar Schrade, a veteran of Colonel Whitney's C Company. "Our war was pretty much over before it started," Schrade said. He looked to Desmond Hamish, a fellow C Company veteran, who nodded in agreement. They had been describing the first days of the Ponga campaign when their company was one of the three spearheads of the initial assault. "Our mortars blew up in the trees or they didn't go off at all. Nothing hit the target area, so our opening barrage was just a wake-up call for the Japs."

Oscar wore an old work shirt that had been ironed. His shoes had been shined. Desmond wore a suit coat over a flannel shirt. A guy from the new vets' museum had come all this way to hear their story. It was a big deal. "The scout leading our platoon was maybe twenty yards ahead of us when a sniper dropped him," Desmond said. "We dove off the path and made a helluva racket shooting into the trees, but all we got was a blizzard of leaves and crap down our necks. The Japs were hidden way the hell up there in the canopy, tied to the trees. They were all around, and we couldn't hardly move without another guy going down. We were just getting organized to make another go of it when our so-called 'flying artillery' bombed us instead of the Japs. I owe this thing to the Army Air Corps," he said, nodding towards the heavy orthopedic shoe on his shortened leg. "And Oscar here, he still got junk in his back. They killed seven of us, wounded twenty more and half-buried everyone else."

Here at the very end of the chain of command was the bloody outcome of decisions made at the top. "In this war the artillery flies," MacArthur had responded when Chandler insisted he would need some of the division's howitzers at Ponga. Thus the division's big guns were left behind in the Outback while rifle companies went into the jungle supported only by mortars and old Australian cannons. Powder charges got wet, fuses were the wrong type, and rounds burst in trees and on bunker roofs. Howitzers could have ripped the bunkers apart from afar, and tanks could have crawled right up and blown them up or burned them out, but General Chandler had been denied both, leaving his attacking soldiers dependent on the air corps – MacArthur's 'flying artillery' – to soften up enemy bunkers. But pilots couldn't even locate their targets, much less bomb them.

In a gated community along the shore of Silver Lake, summer homes sprawled in scented splendor like oiled women on a beach. Spenser found Warren Federer's place in a grove of birches near the golf course. He was a rare find, a lawyer that Chandler had held over from a previous commander's staff to serve as his personal aide.

"It was Murphy's Law run amok," Federer said. He and Spenser sat at opposite ends of a lush leather sofa, Spenser's tape recorder scrolling away on a coffee table between them. A balding fellow with expressive hands and a cordial, self-possessed manner, Federer gave the impression of one accustomed to dealing comfortably with great names and no names alike. He spoke as though from a well-rehearsed script. "Lack of training in patrolling meant rifle companies had a helluva time pinpointing enemy locations. Lack of training in night problems also led to disaster. Whenever a battalion CO tried to launch a surprise attack at night things went wrong from the start. Lack of fire discipline, that sort of thing.

"But so what? Suppose the famous First Infantry Division had been there instead of us. They'd have gotten bogged down too, but instead of all this crap about poor leadership, no guts, and so on – the stuff MacArthur's crowd accused us of – you would have heard about a clever strategy to starve the Jap out. It's all in the telling, and in our case we came from the wrong side of the tracks as far as MacArthur and his pack of regulars were concerned. We were a low-life National Guard division, always a reliable whipping boy when the professionals screw up and look for a scapegoat.

"What happens to a good outfit when the supporting firepower they were trained to expect doesn't show up? When instead of the few hundred sick enemy they discover the hard way that they're up against thousands of fresh troops who are everywhere and nowhere and whose invisibility mocks them? When the only foot trails channel you right into the enemy's killing field? When fever and dread of the jungle suck everything out of you?

"General Chandler was stuck. He had learned from other people's mistakes. Lesson number one was, don't panic. Even with great names breathing down your neck, don't just do something. Do the right thing. So what is the right thing when your boss demands action but doesn't give you the tools for the job? Chandler tried to convince anyone who'd listen – and we had a constant stream of visitors from MacArthur's staff – that we needed our big guns. Only plunging fire from division artillery could break open those bunkers.

"It was a standoff. The navy eventually cut off supply routes to the Japs. Gradually they got sick just like we did, but they were sick and starving too. By the end they were eating their dead. So what was the hurry? Why was MacArthur so desperate for a quick victory? I'll tell you why. He wanted to make a big announcement on December 7th, that's why. It was a publicity stunt. On the first anniversary of Pearl Harbor he'd be splashed all over the front pages. MacArthur strikes back! It was typical MacArthur. It was all about him.

"So on the first of December, General Bagby showed up at the airstrip with a passel of hungry West Point types, and the housecleaning began with a vengeance. MacArthur had put the fear of God into him, and he got right to work kicking ass and getting people killed. Yeah, sure, eventually he took Ponga Station but only because he finally got a couple howitzer tubes and a platoon of Aussie tanks, just what Chandler had been pleading for all along. Even the Aussie general on the scene thought he was crazy, pushing the men the way he did. And then he couldn't get it done by December 7. It took him another two months to burn out the last Jap.

"I asked General Chandler if he knew what he was risking by putting off the frontal attacks MacArthur kept demanding. Of course he did, but he didn't talk about it. During all those weeks when our guys were crawling over the mountains and through the swamps, getting in position, he said over and over that he intended to bring as many of them home as he could. He said it in letters to his wife. I know because I typed them. You have a lot on your mind in a position like that, conflicting priorities and so on, and he was haunted by the butcher's bill we might have to pay. Bagby was different. MacArthur had stripped his mental baggage down to just one thing – take Ponga Station or don't come back."

All this was pay dirt for Spenser. It was the confirmation he'd been seeking all along. Over and over, the men who had lived through the campaign but whose stories never made it into the newspapers or the history books – probably because they undermined the flag-waving nonsense coming from MacArthur's lackeys – were saying the same thing: Ponga Station was a major fuck-up from the top down. No one had told that side of the story yet. Maybe back then journalists couldn't get away with telling the home folks that their sons and brothers had been sacrificed to protect the reputation of a very flawed man. Fifty years later that version, the down and dirty version, was emerging in interview after interview, and Spenser's excitement only increased with Federer's every disclosure.

He handed Federer a photo he had come across of Chandler and Bagby conferring during the Louisiana maneuvers, Chandler compact and wiry, Bagby a towering lummox. They'd been smiling then, old West Point classmates together again as brigadier generals at the dawn of yet another world war. He pressed Federer for details about the showdown between the pair of old friends, both under intense pressure from an aging prima donna but each with his own priorities. Did they argue? Did Chandler go down swinging?

Federer looked at the picture, and when he passed it back he wore a grim smile and was shaking his head. "I was at my field desk in Chandler's headquarters tent. The sides were rolled up. They had stepped outside. I could see them jawing at each other, but I couldn't hear anything. It didn't last long. Somehow Bagby made it clear that he'd been ordered to take command and that Chandler was to pack up and leave. Chandler just tossed his cigarette and walked away. There were no fireworks. I guess all you can do in a situation like that without making things worse is just get out of the way."

Spenser pushed for more. "Did he stand up for himself? Did he say anything to you later or write anything for posterity?" He needed a showdown. He wanted evidence that Chandler went down fighting for the principles he had so eloquently advocated in his *Infantryman* columns.

Federer shrugged. Was he amused by this overwrought fellow and his scattershot questions? "All I know is that the Ponga campaign was never far from his mind. I used to visit him at their home in Ohio. We'd sit on the terrace. He and Annie were martini people but he always had brandy on hand and usually some good steaks too. The division vets' club had presented him with a bronze enlargement of the shoulder patch which he'd set in a place of honor among the flagstones on the terrace. It kept us company along with the smell of steak on the grill. There was a boozy, twilight sense of camaraderie. Anyhow, when Bagby and others came out with their books, Chandler was always the guy who couldn't get the job done – if he was mentioned at all. I begged him to set the story straight. He was a terrific writer. He could have spun a wonderful tale and a valuable one, but it just wasn't his style. He couldn't blow his own horn.

"He and General Marshall were friends from their China days together back in the thirties. Through the years Marshall compiled a list of up and comers to command divisions if war came again and the army was expanded. You can bet Chandler was on it, but Marshall warned him not to take on a National Guard division. He said they were tainted by home state politics and weak leadership. A new commander would have to clean house, and that would stir up resentment in the state capitol. You start kicking out the dead wood, and that pisses off the governor and legislators and hometown editors. The bitching starts and never lets up. The job had been a career killer for too many promising regular army officers. Marshall told him to hold out for a draftee division, but Chandler thought he could deal with all that, so when he was offered the Bold Eagle he took us on anyway, and at first everything was great. The men loved him and so did his staff. He didn't clean house but went easy on long-serving home state officers. They were his team and he was determined to work with them, but to MacArthur that was proof that he was too soft. Once the division went into combat he was a marked man.

"West Point reunions could be tough, but he never missed one. He was among the last of his class still able to show up. You can imagine him lifting his glass to those missing and present and no doubt to good fellowship, sharp wit, good drink, and all that. But you know what some Pentagon big shot scrawled in his 201 File? 'Moral coward', that's what. Can you imagine that?

"Bold Eagle reunions were bittersweet too, though he was always the star. A roar went up whenever he entered the room. Bagby came once to give a talk. At least he tried. It took guts. I'll credit him for that. He was contrite. He admitted he'd been too hard on the division at first and that it took time for him to realize what they'd been up against all along. But the men wouldn't let him finish.

A shout went up: 'Bodybagby! Bodybagby!' and he was drowned out. That was the last we saw of him."

In the overheated dining room of a farmhouse turned assisted living facility outside of Plum City, Spenser sat across the table from an old fellow named Milan Lucas. "Skeeter Creek was where General Bagby made his first appearance at the front. Of course we hated him, the poor sap – 'Bodybagby' and all that – but looking back I almost feel sorry for the guy." Milan's voice was like a bowling ball rumbling down a gutter. Truck traffic on the overpass nearby roared like a waterfall in the background.

A droopy face, a big goofy smile, a slow, easy manner. "He stood in full view of God and all and told us flat out that back over the mountains they said we had no guts, that they were calling us the nightcrawlers because we only came out of our holes when we got soaked, and by god that was gonna change right now. We were gonna fight, and it started right now. We'd get our asses across that fucking creek and in among those fucking bunkers and blow them to hell up, and he started pointing at people... you... you... That sort of thing. I was first sergeant by then. So I figured what the hell, someone has to be the first one into the soup. I took a rope and slid down into the creek and swam across. I tied the rope to a big root and others came along pulling themselves hand over hand. Pretty soon I had a wounded guy hanging on my back, and I got careless and caught a round in the fleshy part of my arm, but the others climbed up sopping wet and disappeared into the grass. Grenades went off. There was a big ruckus. Another rope was strung and more guys slogged by.

"Never did find out what happened to those guys, but later an after-action team went over the site and came up with a theory. A dozen or so made it through the high grass to the first line of bunkers. Lots of dead Japs and our guys too showed what happened. The rest made it to a sandy clearing but not to the grassy berm a couple hundred yards beyond. Probably they were out of grenades and low on ammo. Their walky-talky was beyond effective range if ever it worked at all, which was rare. Strange how the earth sucked them in, a hand poking out here, a booted foot there, a half-buried helmet. That was Bagby for you. Had to get going before we were good and ready. No reinforcements, no way to resupply the guys who got where they did. They were easy pickings for Japs on the other side of that berm."

A bachelor farmer named Digger Vrba had tried to dodge him by hiding out in a shed, but once Spenser tracked him down he wouldn't stop talking: "The Jap was great for keeping diaries. They was real tight about records and stuff. A guy I nailed flopped out of the tree dangling from a rope, and I come on his diary. The boys give the book up to intelligence, and in there he put a record of our guys he shot, seven by number. I'd been scouting them snipers day by day, but they was everywhere and nowhere – out of sight way the hell up in the canopy, down amongst them big greasy roots, always so blended into the slick and the slime you'd hardly catch a glimpse. I give you a copy of what he wrote, some of it, but put into English so's you can put that up on a wall."

Later, walking Spenser to the car: "The down and dirty

was our piece of the war. The glory boys, they come along later with all their fleets of shiny bombers and big tanks, their fancy jackets and jump boots and cocky faces, not us make-do early boys all wasted and haunted in our raggedy monkey suits. People don't want to hear about the shaky times, only the glory times."

* * *

So it went until winter put an end to Spenser's life on the road. By then Chandler had become an obsession. Displays for everything else would fall into place. Timelines and the materials to bring them to life could be pieced together from the mounds of stuff yet to be sorted and catalogued or acquired from army sources. But for Spenser, Chandler was the beating heart of the story – a mystery and an inspiration. It was what he had not done, the orders he refused to obey in spite of enormous pressure, and his maddening silence ever after, that made him such a tragic and mysterious figure. The whole campaign was a tragedy but not only because it had bled the division dry. The tragedy Spenser had in mind had never even been acknowledged, much less put before the public: an enlightened concept of small arms combat that put a greater value on the lives of citizen soldiers than on blind obedience to higher authority had been buried, repudiated, erased from the record in Papua, and buried with it was the career of the man who had preached that concept.

Back at the museum Spenser was overwhelmed. So much to do. It was stressful but never felt like work, and the full-time staff at New Camp was eager to pitch in. Whether civilian or military they wanted in on this big new project. To them Spenser became 'the museum guy', a minor celebrity to people at headquarters, the mail room, the PX and the commissary. Need photos or documents blown up and mounted on display board? Signs made? Lighting fixtures for display cases? More wall outlets? Someone on post would come through.

For the first time ever making decisions – executive decisions, no less – was not a hand-wringing chore. No one was looking over his shoulder. Old Building One felt like home. It was where he was *supposed* to be. He was uncovering a long-buried story and correcting an historic injustice. When he was on the road, it almost seemed as though the vets and their wives had been waiting all these years for him to show up so they could finally unload, setting before him scrapbooks and photo albums and shoe boxes full of wartime letters they had been hoarding for just such an occasion. That part of their lives had been locked away for half a century, but he was the guy with the secret code, the one they could finally open up to.

One night he dreamed he was in a cafeteria. His tray was very heavy and hard to balance. The tables were full. People coming and going bumped him, sending glasses on his tray sliding towards the edges, and he panicked, terrified of making a scene. At the only table with empty chairs, Mrs Neumann was in deep conversation with a murky figure lost in cigarette smoke. His old taxi driver come back to life? But no, suddenly sunlight flooded the room, revealing a pretty young woman in a party dress.

Mrs Neumann appeared to be consoling her. The girl was looking at him, so sad, so blue. He wanted to join them but couldn't move, terrified of being drawn back into the dense floral heat of those two, the hothouse vapors that had so addled him before... His heart would break, the tray would fall. Already he was sucking air, his heart pounding, his knees giving way, silverware and crockery slipping and sliding, the glasses tipping over the edge... Oh, the shame and longing!

He woke in a panic, gasping and sweaty and too late. His underpants were sticky, the sheet stained.

Ah well, no big deal. He sat on the side of the bed. Such paralyzing dread and longing were old companions from an earlier life. At least now they could only visit in dreams, and he was okay. His new mission had liberated him from all that. To scare off his ghosts all he had to do was remember that now he had a story to tell. He was a changed man.

The heater glowed in its corner. He dialled it down and paced in his dark little office until he was dry but shivering. Then he crawled back under the blankets and slept like a baby.

He wrote a story for *The Stalker* urging hometown buddies to gather in small groups to recall and record their war. He prescribed the whole procedure – siting the microphone, shutting out background noise, and he urged them to speak up and AR-TIC-U-LATE because everything they said would be transcribed and indexed and preserved for all time. Was any other shoe-string vets' museum across the country casting such a wide net?

Women from the auxiliary began to show up, tough old birds most of them, and they didn't want to sit around. They wanted to contribute something meaningful. Soon he had them sorting old clothes and web gear, separating good stuff from junk, even taking home exhibit quality items to clean and press. They robbed buttons, insignia and even shoelaces from the junk to complete a khaki shirt, a class A jacket, a pair of dress shoes. When cassette tapes started to trickle in, headquarters lent him typewriters and recorders, and soon four of the women were wearing headphones and tapping away. Others brought tape measures and masking tape from home and set to work marking off sections of the floor and walls using a floor plan that he had sketched. He told them he needed to enlist their retiree husbands with carpentry and mechanical backgrounds for projects coming up in the months ahead. Let the word go forth: skilled volunteers needed!

Would he have enough displays in place to justify a grand opening next summer? The fiftieth anniversary of the call-up of the Bold Eagle Division was not far off. He imagined an open house in the spruced up officers' club in New Camp, with invitations going out to the old boys and their families as well as the media. A buffet meal, couples dancing to wartime favorites played by the Guard band, a speaker or two and a message sent around the state: Help preserve the Bold Eagle story! Don't let the Pentagon bury our proud heritage! Get to know what your fathers *really* did in the war!

He needed to lay before the trustees a fixed plan. From the start he had to win them over to his version of the story.

If he failed to take charge right off, if he wobbled, if he went after some wishy-washy consensus he risked stagnation, endless committee meetings and a constant drip, drip of off-the-wall 'inspirations' to contend with but no clarity, no compelling narrative. The result would please no one. The place needed a message. It had to tell a story, and he must persuade them that the perfect symbol of that story was General Graham Chandler, the unacknowledged hero who sabotaged his own career to shield his raw Bold Eagle soldiers from the reckless demands of a self-absorbed theater commander.

For weeks he stewed over how to parcel out the division's history over the available space. Simplicity won out. The early years – post-civil war through World War One – would occupy the bar-room, or Gallery One, as he called it. Gallery Three would remain as it was – closed to the public and devoted to storage and space for preparing exhibits. It was the big central room, Gallery Two, that would carry the heart of the story, starting with the division's post-World War One doldrums and the Depression era, but concentrating on the opening phase of the US Army's offensive in the Pacific when the unseasoned, underequipped Bold Eagle division was fed piecemeal into war at its most primitive and bewildering – the Ponga campaign. This was the role congress had envisioned for the National Guard decades ago – to buy time resisting the enemy while the nation mobilized to destroy him.

Several times a day the shriek of low flying fighter jets interrupted his thoughts, though where they came from remained a mystery until a cashier at the commissary told him about an Air Guard installation hidden in another corner of the wilderness training grounds, a virtual mock-up of a NATO forward air strip complete with camouflaged bunkers. Camp Palmer was full of secrets, and some of them were very noisy.

Though he'd been on the job barely two months, so immersed had he become that Germany, Mrs Neumann, and his fall from grace seemed from another era, remote and almost insignificant. Finally he was living the life he was meant for, and he was exhilarated. He was isolated but not alone, not as long as General Chandler and the maligned Bold Eagle were on his mind.

On a Saturday in mid-November the trustees came trooping in with wives in tow until all twelve were gathered around bar-room tables jammed together in Gallery One, still redolent of its bar-room era, beery flooring, dangling saber jets and all. Spenser had stripped his office/bedroom of personal gear, converting it back into a kitchen, and the wives swarmed in two by two toting pots of chilli and beans and mini-wieners swimming in barbecue sauce, plus pies and a sheet cake. Soon a coffee pot was gurgling away. The women carried on conversations from the last reunion or fundraiser or committee meeting. You would think they owned the place.

In spite of sweaty palms and a dry-as-dust mouth, Spenser willed himself to enter Gallery One as the man in charge. The old guys in their Saturday jeans and flannel shirts were jawing about pals he would never meet and experiences Spenser could never be part of, but he did not hesitate. He took a seat, slapped his open palm on the table and called them to order. He had brooded over how they would size him up. If they took him for a reject from a distant installation eager to unload its pet misfit, he was dead. He had to gain their respect right off, and so far at least he certainly had their attention.

"Gentlemen, I am John Spenser, and I am thrilled to be the new executive officer of the Bold Eagle Museum. I have studied your history. I intend to tell your story as it has never been told before. We have a big job ahead of us. Let's get to work."

He was off, handing out copies of his draft mission statement, then a sketch of his floorplan, then an outline of goals to be met along the way to the grand opening. He hovered over them passing papers faster than they could keep up, meanwhile launching into a description of his oral history project and the work the ladies were doing sorting and sewing and transcribing... He wanted to knock them silly with all he had been up to, how on-the-ball their new guy was, how they needn't bother trying to keep up. It was enough for them to know that their museum was in good hands.

As they gazed from one handout to the next some did appear overwhelmed, others mildly interested, and a few let him know with their eyes that they were unimpressed by his eager-beaver performance. He was telling them why Gallery Two, the big room, would be home to their war, the Pacific war, with the Ponga campaign the heart and soul of the story, and above all why General Chandler would be the stand-out figure, the guy who stood for all of them and the dilemma they'd been plunged into. That in turn set him off reviewing the whole complicated picture, one regiment trudging over mountains where no white man had gone before, another ferried by C-47s to a grassy airstrip, and a third chancing sea passage in primitive cargo boats dodging strafing runs by Japanese fighters, the scattered division sweating and sickening for weeks in stinking muck until finally in position for coordinated assaults on the Japanese perimeter, only to find themselves funneled into killing zones manned by a fresh, virtually invisible enemy

Spenser had worked himself into a sweat, but when he looked up from his notes he did not see his own excitement reflected in their faces. They gazed at each other across the table or fiddled with their handouts or looked on with the weary gaze of high school kids whose minds were elsewhere. It dawned on him that he was taking too much for granted. He was caught up in the drama of the big picture whereas their personal experiences had been chaotic and fragmentary. They knew their war like a flea knows a dog, intimately but not well. He might be the 'expert' but they were only grudgingly his students. After all, they had lived it and he had not. No wonder he was losing them.

But maybe this was as it should be. It served his purpose and theirs. They would get their museum, and it would tell *his* version of their war.

The scent of barbecue sauce came to his rescue. Wives appeared bearing pots and platters. Museum business gave way to food, fellowship, a room brought back to life.

Not only had he survived, he had prevailed. He grabbed a plate and joined the feast.

Later a cheerful voice called to him from across the table: "Yeah, but what if he was praying to be bailed out? Chandler, I mean. He was in a helluva jam. And what if Bagby was the answer to his prayers?" Spenser put down his fork. Was this a joke? Some of the others seemed to think so. They looked to him for a response. He didn't have one.

"Just wait," he said finally. "You'll see."

Weeks later he was alone in the snowbound building. It felt like an outpost on the moon. Frost blurred the windows. His breath steamed whenever he emerged from the heated kitchen into the great dark hall that was Gallery Two. Even in army boots and a heavy army parka he could not escape the cold. Yet he was busy, at peace, still exhilarated – high on his freedom to create a world of his own. Day after day he went about painstakingly laying out exhibits in old glass display cases salvaged from the museum at West Point. Confined on hands and knees between walls of heavy plate glass, fumbling silver pushpins from a box on the floor, he mounted photos, maps, photocopied scrapbook pages and newspaper clippings. His glowing capsule was like a space ship. His pulse thundered in his ears. Was he running out of oxygen? If he collapsed would anyone find him? Would he end up on display, a crumpled blue GI sealed in an iceberg?

Adrift with him on this eerie voyage was General Graham Chandler, for it was the Chandler exhibit that was closest to his heart. The division's early history – World

War One, the between war decades and so on – could wait. He was obliged to tell the complete story, but first he had to be satisfied with the depiction of Chandler, the unacknowledged hero.

So front and center went the army headshot taken after Chandler's promotion to major general. Also one of Chandler in helmet and combat gear, an '03 Springfield across his lap, sitting on the top step of a jungle hootch with junior members of his staff clutching their weapons. They are young, eager and proud, like a high school football team. Chandler, their coach and mentor, eyes them warily as though he knows what lay ahead. Then up goes a shot of Graham Chandler, senior citizen, in sports jacket and tie, reaching out to shake hands at a Bold Eagle reunion in the late 1950s.

But of most importance to Spenser was a hand-lettered list of 'lessons learned' from Chandler's study of the army's performance in World War One, boiled down from his *Infantryman* columns of the mid-1930s:

Panic rolls downhill. Stay out of its way... Work with the team that has trained together. Don't try to assemble a group of all-stars... You don't drive nails with your fist, so don't send your soldiers against fixed emplacements unless they have the tools to succeed, and so on.

Opposite each were orders from MacArthur that turned the Ponga campaign into a repeat of the army's World War One fiascos: *Take Ponga or don't come back... Fire Chandler. Fire his deadweight commanders. Replace them all... Do it now! Whatever it takes!*

The upshot of MacArthur's rage and panic? A

prudent, enlightened division commander was sidelined for the rest of the war, his reputation in tatters, his soldiers wasted in a succession of futile assaults, and eventually a hollow victory that would have fallen into the division's hands anyway but for the celebrity general's 'Do it now!' mindset.

Here in a rough old frontier building Chandler was finally getting his due while the supposed heroes of the campaign, MacArthur and his factotum Bagby, would be exposed as panicky hotheads. For his loyalty Bagby had been rewarded with a fourth star and, years later, high praise for a memoir depicting himself as a fearless, whatever-it-takes kind of guy. What Spenser was documenting for a long-misled public was belated vindication of the forgotten man who had answered a higher calling and had been written out of the story for his trouble.

Still, something was missing. He did not have a rock solid answer for doubters like the old vet at the trustee meeting. If only Chandler had made the case for himself. Was he too proud? Too much of a team player? Or simply resolved to do the right thing no matter the personal cost? Laboring in solitude, Spenser half convinced himself that he was along on one of those patio cook-outs at that big old house in Ohio. They are relaxing on lawn chairs, drinks in hand. The smell of grilling steak is in the autumn air as they carry on about the old days and the old team, but an unacknowledged melancholy burdens the conversation, until finally Spenser confesses what has been on his mind forever:

"General, you've got to write your side of the story. You're a helluva writer. You'd set the record straight once and for all."

But Chandler just draws on his cigarette and says, "Well, you know, I never went in for that sort of thing..."

One night with the space heater humming away and blankets weighing on him, Spenser crept through a steam bath of a jungle, scared to death. His last link to humanity was the figure lurking over him, protecting him. He was Private Low, stuck to the ground, barely able to creep along, and that protective shadow was thrown by Sergeant High. They were in this nightmare together, come what may.

Even before toast and coffee the next morning he sketched the scene. He went back to it again and again over the next few days, reworking it and repositioning the figures until they were just right – crouching one above the other, brutish and dark, their faces fever-colored under sweat-streaked grime. Sergeant High searches tree tops while Private Low scours the underbrush. They ooze through the muck, spring-loaded, conjoined lumps, poised to strike.

He called the university art department. A pair of grad students called back, and a few days later they showed up in paint-spattered overalls and sweatshirts. They hauled in bedrolls, tarps, pails, and heavy sacks of some kind of powdered stuff. Spenser hid out in his office while the newcomers' loud music, loud voices, and mysterious thunks and bangs took over Gallery Two. His desk was piled with scrapbooks, bundled letters and his own notes and sketches. Leaning against the wall were the misty, autumn-hued recollections of a long-gone colonel rendered in oil on canvas: a blacksmith shoeing a horse, officers on the pistol range, young soldiers gathered around a campfire. Spread open before him were pages of yellowed newsprint: *Radio Call – South Australia's Radio Weekly*: Bold Eagle musicians in moody Hollywood poses, a trio of trumpeters, a quartet of crooners, a blissed-out drummer. *US Army Swing Band in Action*, read the headline. American music played by American soldiers. Further proof for the Aussies that the cavalry had arrived.

He had calls to make – to the map guy at headquarters who was putting together a giant replica of the Ponga front that would serve as graphic background to the displays. And to the sign shop where they were stencilling BOLD EAGLE MEMORIAL MUSEUM AND ARCHIVES onto a tin panel to hang over the front door.

All in good time. For now he stretched out in his chair and wove his fingers behind his head. He thought back on all he had accomplished in a couple of months. It warmed his heart. Glowing from within like blocks of ice, display cases lined in rows told the story of the Bold Eagle division from the last bloody assaults on the Hindenburg Line in 1918 to the mid-Depression era of skinny-chested, gap-toothed teenagers with soup-bowl haircuts. In one Old Camp photo their oversized fatigues hang from them like washing on the line as they gather around a Browning water-cooled, tripod-mounted, kraut killer of a machine gun, a genuine nicked-up piece of history still as deadly as it had been twenty years earlier on the Western Front. It stood in the grass like a brooding Doberman surrounded by dimwits and goof-offs. So much innocence, so much potential mayhem, here in a pocket of wilderness in the middle of nowhere. In other photos they're playing softball, lined up for supper with mess kits in hand, and drilling on an armory floor in mid-winter. History, camaraderie, a sense of mission throughout years of bleakness and isolation.

Then on to the call-up and the great showdown at Ponga Station, where, tragically, once again panicky demands from an out-of-touch commander led to needless casualties, and where one good man paid the price for resisting.

It was the Bold Eagle story as he saw it, and it was just version one. When the public and media and business communities got a glimpse of what was going on in the old lodge he expected more and bigger donations than they'd ever get from a thousand bake sales, raffles, and bingo tournaments. Then he could afford to dream big – dioramas, headphones playing audio clips from his interviews... Meanwhile the grad students' project underway in Gallery Two gave off a pleasant chemical smell like the airplane dope of his boyhood projects.

1989

THAT LUMINOUS WAFER SUSPENDED ABOVE THE stream of tail lights ahead had to be one of those places called an oasis. About damn time. Jack Hagan was desperate. He was trapped in a flood of lights drawing him ever closer to O'Hare and the point of no return. An oasis was exactly what he needed. The sky was an ominous bruise and the bruise was deepening, spreading. Everything was coming at him too fast. He needed to break away and hide out for a spell before it was too late. He had to settle things in his mind while there was still time, and he was desperate to pee.

The ramp curved up to a cement plateau which in turn directed him, now on foot, into a lighted island of benevolent lassitude. Children crawled through an Enchanted Forest of plastic. Grown-ups dipped fries into catsup. Underneath the lounging and chewing and dull-eyed gazing, bright rivers of homebound and outbound traffic snaked into the distance.

Two sailors headed into the men's room, and Hagan

was right behind them. He settled over a urinal midway between them. He closed his eyes, moaning and tremoring. It felt so good yet burned so bad.

When he opened his eyes he realized that he had drawn their attention, probably because of all his splashing and moaning. Hagan knew kids from high school who had gone through basic at the nearby naval training center fifty years ago when the navy was fighting wars on both oceans. "Just out of basic, are you?" he said. "Done with all that bullshit? Now if only the navy keeps its end of the bargain and shows you the world like they promised. Back in my day we all did our bit, not like kids nowadays, too busy spending money they didn't earn and too chicken to take risks. Another time and place I'd buy you guys a beer."

He heard them talking as they washed their hands. On their way out the door they were laughing. He still waited, wobble-legged and light-headed, for the last drop.

He ordered a salad, two cheeseburgers, and a Coke, and settled at a table midway between northbound and southbound traffic. What a fool he had been. All it had taken was a few martinis and a name in a newsletter. Old friends would embrace him. John's mother would have mellowed and at least acknowledged him. There would be a measure of forgiveness, maybe even a recollection of mutual affection back when they were ruled by a sense of now or never. He'd always been a charmer. He'd find a way. And of course he and Johnny would meet man to man like old mates. There would be much to explain but also much to share, a table full of bottles and promises to be in touch – as friends if not father and son. It would be a grand return, old grievances would fall away, absolution, resolution, affection even. It was a dream that had put a lump in his throat. "What a disgusting old slobber you've become," Honora would have scolded, handing him a tissue. "Wipe your face."

He had set a trap for himself and blissfully stumbled into it. And he'd been paying the price ever since. But what did it mean, this cascade of rejections and humiliations? In the old days people dressed like peons and washed up once or twice a week, yet they had fun, they took risks, they were unafraid. There had been so much to look forward to. Nowadays everyone was squeaky clean and smelled like cinnamon buns but seemed to be hiding out and nursing grievances. What was behind this comeuppance? Was it payback for crimes committed and obligations shirked? An obstacle course inflicted by the gods to make him earn his way back to his son? In fleeing to O'Hare and a long flight home was he failing the test? Would he hate himself if he left now?

His salad and one cheeseburger were gone, but he'd need another Coke to get down the second burger. He gathered his trash and was about to step away from the table when he spotted the two sailors. They were in shadows near the exit, talking to a policeman. A moment later they were out the door, and the policeman appeared to be scowling across the busy dining area to where Jack stood with his handful of garbage.

He collapsed onto his chair. This was nuts. Un-fucking believable. The sight of the remaining burger turned his stomach. It took him a blurry moment to transition from sick to angry. Suddenly he was back on his feet, forcing a big bold smile, and marching through the foot traffic to the cop. "A very good evening to you, Officer. You look concerned. Do you have business with me?"

The officer was not pleased. "Cruising for sailors, are you? At a McDonald's of all places?"

Jack could only stare, dumbfounded. Then something inside him went slack. Slowly he started for the exit. The policeman fell into step beside him, as though to shield the men's room from him.

1989

———

SPENSER FELL ASLEEP TO THE CREAK OF SHIFTING timbers and woke to the metronomic splat of melting ice. The Lodge was a megaphone amplifying sounds of the thaw. By ones and twos the ladies reappeared in winter coats and galoshes. They brought their own snacks. He provided coffee from an ancient percolator and put them to work stuffing and addressing envelopes. Invitations to the open house were on the way. There was no turning back.

So much to do, so little time. He had grown up with a legend of an unknowable father who had given his life in a mission that he'd known would never be revealed. It was as though his very existence had been erased from history. You can't be more dedicated to your country than that. For Spenser, Chandler was the personification of that same legend, sacrificing career and reputation in an effort to spare his soldiers needless suffering. Best of all, unlike his missing father, Chandler was knowable, a man with ideas and feelings as reflected in his paper trail. In effect,

Chandler was the guy Spenser had been looking for all along. In a few months the public would be introduced to a story of great peril in which the central players were men from their own neighborhoods and a forgotten general who championed their welfare over his own career. What a tale!

But so much yet to do to bring that tale to life! Picky stuff Spenser had been putting off all winter suddenly loomed large. He had to come up with a press release – hell, a series of them – good enough to attract television and newspaper coverage. The caterer had been lukewarm from the beginning and backed out in April. June was his month – weddings, graduations, etc. Camp Palmer was too far away for too little in return. The old Spenser would have panicked. The new Spenser just called the commander of an upstate mess unit who jumped at the opportunity to show the old-timers how well today's soldiers ate in the field. Problem solved. Still there was plenty to worry about. Had the band leader put together a program of the right kind of music? Were his musicians up to the task? Down the road he'd need to write a draft constitution, settle on a cataloguing system, generate operating agreements...

The one job he looked forward to was digging through the remaining scrapbooks and cartons of photos. Scrapbooks were tedious to contemplate in their bulk but hard to put down when open on his desk. He felt a sense of companionship with the mother or sister who, year after year, had spent evenings searching the local paper with scissors in hand, scouting out stories of hometown boys in training and at war. Collectively they had rescued from the trash heap a story of the division that was much more than a compilation of dispatches from the battlefield. The Bold Eagle of the scrapbooks was a community. It was softball and boxing matches, cook-outs, dances, even drinking parties in the hills of Old Camp, the booze confiscated by officers who, in civilian life, happened to be prohibition agents. It was hunting buddies and high school teammates going off to summer camp together. Through the dark years of the Depression, membership in the Bold Eagle was a reminder that even in the most remote and grim and suffering little towns, you and your buddies were linked to the wider world and to history.

As RSVPs came in, the ladies went to work lettering Bold Eagle nametags. The facilities people at New Camp promised Spenser a spic-and-span officers' club and the band director an afternoon soaked in forties' nostalgia.

The sky cleared. A faint green haze emerged over coffee-colored fields. On his way to the dumpster one morning he spotted figures in orange vests and tin hats far off in the grassy basin under Target Bluff, trudging along with surveying gear over their shoulders. They had to be reservists from an engineer unit, he decided – New Camp's first trainees of the year. Guard units and reservists throughout the Midwest would be preparing for their annual trek to New Camp for field training. It struck Spenser as awfully early given how soggy woods and fields remained, but what else could those guys in orange vests be but harbingers of a new training cycle?

One day there was a knock on his door. He opened it

and immediately felt a rush of guilt. He should know this woman but he couldn't place her. "Mr Spenser, I'm Louise? I showed you around that day?"

"Oh sure. Louise. How...?"

"I heard you got some volunteers working here, so I wondered if I could pitch in too. I thought maybe you'd let me know." Louise – the one who had waited in vain for her brother's buddies to pay a visit after the war, the one who cleaned up the lodge and showed Spenser around on his first day. The one who wanted to help out in some way, to be remembered. Spenser had forgotten all about her.

"Louise! Of course. You bet. Follow me."

In the cupboard he found paper towels and a bottle of Windex, and while she went to work on the display cases he told her about the open house. He'd need a hand that day for sure. She assured him that he could count on her.

* * *

As early morning mist melted away, that June Saturday at Old Fort emerged bright, proud and country fresh, as though custom-made for an exalted occasion. For Spenser the next twelve hours passed in a blur. With Louise occupying the sign-in table at the museum he was free to follow his impulses. The field mess outfit had pulled into New Camp the night before. Their big green vehicles were stashed out of sight behind the officers' club when Spenser showed up next morning, but there was no hiding all the clashing and clanging going on in the kitchen. Inside, the old wooden floor glistened with a fresh coat of wax. Starched tablecloths had already been draped over tables in the banquet hall. The facilities people had come through.

As visitors trickled in, Spenser was there to lend a guiding hand. He spent much of the afternoon leading convoys of the curious along back roads, past warehouses and blocks of barracks, out of New Camp into the training grounds. Pasture-like fields and wooded hills scrolled away into the horizon. Signposts appeared by dirt trails leading into the bush: 'Hand Grenade Range... Drop Zone ... Medical Simulation Training Facility' and so on, reminding old-timers of a world of crushed pine, torn earth and spent powder, the odors of life in the field, army style. A sharp turn south sent them rumbling over multiple sets of train tracks, through ranks of white pine planted by CCC boys over half a century ago, out into the vast, sun-drenched hideaway of Old Camp, its fields rippling away to Target Bluff in the west and wooded hills to the south and east. Then down the dirt road and up the hillside to famous Building One and an encounter with their own Bold Eagle history. They knew that for many of them this would be the last time.

Arriving back at the officers' club Spenser heard a brassy Glen Miller hit, or was it Benny Goodman? Inside he watched old boys get dragged onto the dance floor. The food was *first rate...*, someone's wife told him, and the music was *heavenly!... great fun!...*, the toasts and tributes *so moving, so heartfelt.*

On a later visit to the museum Louise whispered that visitors were saying wonderful things and that the full-sized mock-up of Sergeant High and Private Low was a big hit. Nervous exhaustion had left him winded. He leaned against the porch railing and allowed himself a moment of self-congratulation. If they liked what they were seeing today, just wait until they laid eyes on the permanent installations to follow. All he needed was money and time.

The sun touched the edge of Target Bluff, lighting up the ridge of raggedy pines and throwing the whole grassy basin into shadow. Spenser turned away from the light just as Louise handed him the guest book. "It's almost full," she said. "That's a lot of people. Now I have to get home before dark."

As she walked off Spenser muttered her name. He couldn't forget it again, couldn't let her feel ignored again. Spenser's gaze drifted to a dust-colored sedan parked at a distance from his pickup. He hadn't noticed it before. He was feeling good. The guest book was a gold mine of potential donors who would go home, speak well of the museum and generate even more donors. TV crews had caught some of the officers' club nostalgia, plus glimpses of the Ponga display and Sergeant High and Private Low. Let the word go forth, he thought.

After a last glance at the sinking sun he went in search of the lingering party.

A couple was standing by the Ponga display. As Spenser approached, the woman abruptly left her husband's side and started for the exit, walking fast and avoiding eye contact.

The man was too young to be a Bold Eagle old-timer. "I'd guess you're the guy running the show," he said, offering his hand. His smile was cool, businesslike.

"I guess I am. John Spenser."

"Just the man I want to see. I'm Dave Benbow. On leave from the Pentagon. My dad has been filling me in about what you got going on here."

For the moment Spenser was more interested in the speaker's credentials. "You must be a full-timer."

"I am. Just sweated out my last month at a desk. Next stop is Fort Hood where I'll take over a tank battalion. My father was one of the very few Bold Eagle riflemen to see it all, from the Ponga fiasco to the Japanese surrender on Luzon."

Wow. Spenser took a deep breath. "That's very impressive. Impressive credentials for both of you. A tank battalion is a big deal. And not many ground-pounders made it through the whole Pacific war."

"He was there when Yamashita turned over his sword. So you can imagine what the Bold Eagle means to him. He and his pals have some issues with what you've put together here." They were both in civvies, but Benbow struck Spenser as someone who was always in uniform no matter what he was wearing. Spenser knew those eyes: the casual manner was misleading. "They're uneasy about the way you've handled the Chandler-Bagby business. After looking into it, so am I. I hope you have a few minutes to hear me out."

Exhausted from the events of the day, Spenser was also hungry, thirsty – and, suddenly, very uncomfortable. He did not like where this was headed.

"I guess I can't be surprised if I've stirred the pot a little. But let's sit down in Gallery One." He offered Benbow a warm Coke or leftover coffee. Benbow settled for water in a paper cup like Spenser was having.

Like a good staff officer, he had done his homework. He might not have read the official history front to back, but he had boned up somehow, and he got right to the point. He was disappointed. Spenser's focus on the generals was misplaced. It overshadowed the soldiers' story. In insisting that General Chandler made a conscious decision to protect his soldiers from MacArthur, Spenser was engaging in wishful thinking. So Chandler had written articles about tactical blunders and command shortcomings during the First World War. So what? Where was the evidence that these rather pedestrian 'lessons learned' had morphed into a vision so compelling that it took precedence over the urgent orders of the theater commander? Isn't it just as likely that he had come up against a brick wall? That he was stuck, out of steam and out of ideas? Wouldn't it make sense in that situation for the theater commander to replace him with someone fresh?

"Don't you think," Benbow said quietly, evenly, as though to soft pedal a hard lesson, "that maybe your enthusiasm for one man's laudable concern for his soldiers has driven you off the track? Shouldn't the museum be about what actually happened, not what might have been? Shouldn't the spotlight be on the soldiers and their stories? Shouldn't they be depicted as victors rather than victims?"

These were hard blows. Spenser waited for them to sink in, but they had him wobbling. "Well sure, Colonel," he said finally. "That's one side of the story, the side told by MacArthur and his people. I think there's more to the story, an important angle that's been left out till now. General Chandler didn't give up. He pressed his battalion commanders to keep up the pressure, urging them to patrol aggressively, seek out gaps in the Japanese lines..."

"Which to the troops meant what? You've read about patrols that went out a short distance and hid the rest of the day. What does that tell you? They knew things were shaky at the top. This wasn't the walkover it was supposed to be. They weren't going to take risks if they suspected it was already a botched job. An infantry division on the offensive is a dynamic machine. If it sputters to a stop, someone has to fire it up again and fast. If current leadership isn't up to the job, then the sooner someone else takes over, the better."

Faced with such a head-on attack, Spenser faltered. Words eluded him. This guy was a professional. He'd been to all the advanced schools. He seemed to be on the fast track to bigger things. Spenser damned his paralysis. The clock was ticking. This was only his first time on the defensive. More criticism from high places was bound to be coming. "To me, the question is: what did Bagby and his team accomplish and at what cost? We could take up the whole museum with tales of combat, hell in the jungle and all that, but so what?" There! That felt good. He liked what he was hearing. He straightened his back and dared to look Colonel Benbow in the eye. "The question remains: was it necessary? Bagby didn't succeed until he got what Chandler had been begging for all along – tanks and a few big guns. And until the Japs were already half-starved and sick to death. Chandler had preached patience, but panic won the day thanks to MacArthur and Bagby. No wonder the division returned to Australia a spent force. It didn't have to be that way. That's the side of the story the army neglects, and that's why we're telling it here. As Chandler warned years earlier, 'Don't repeat failure.'"

From time to time Benbow nodded in apparent agreement. Sunlight through the western windows had lit up the back of his head. Soon it would be in Spenser's eyes. "Okay. Benefit of the doubt. Let's assume Chandler had altruistic motives. That makes for an appealing story and a fresh perspective, I agree. A highly regarded guy goes down fighting. He plays by the rules he learned from the last war and it costs him. Even the grandiose buffoon who fired him later acknowledges the error of his ways, vindicating your fallen hero. Very provocative, against the grain, and so on. But that's not the real story. That's a daydream. That's a maybe. The real story is what actually *did* happen on the ground. Under Bagby our guys put up a helluva fight and ultimately prevailed. Let's give them their due.

"Put yourself in Bagby's shoes. 'Take Ponga or don't come back!' Imagine flying into battle with an order like that ringing in your ears. And what did he find when he got there? Unit commanders who were out of their depth. Demoralized soldiers huddling behind the lines. And among those still up front, an attitude of don't shoot them and they won't shoot us. From where I sit it's as though you've hitched your wagon to a pet theory, and it's blinded you to the big picture. Yes, sure, General Chandler was loyal to his troops, loyal to a fault some would say, but his refusal to act decisively put Bagby in a helluva bind. You know, there's another old saying to consider: 'the fog of war.'"

Benbow glanced at his watch. He had not touched his water. The guy was a cool customer. Spenser's cup was empty, but even so he could barely unstick his tongue from the roof of his mouth. He was not a cool customer. He was tremoring with fatigue.

"You have a terrific opportunity here," Benbow said. "A terrific chance to do right by an outfit that never got the recognition it deserved."

Spenser shaded his eyes. "I think I'm doing exactly that. We're standing up for a guy who was humiliated for doing the right thing. Chandler was leading an army of citizen soldiers, not a bunch of bullied peasants like the enemy. To him every soldier was a free man on loan to the army. He had rights. He shouldn't have to risk death just to satisfy a superior's vanity. If heavy weapons could do the job from a distance, don't waste soldiers in an assault. If starving the enemy out was an option, even if it took longer, that was better than wasting soldiers..."

He knew he was out on a limb. He felt hollowed out, cornered.

"Look," Benbow said wearily. "You can tell it the way it was, ugliness and all, or you can settle for the Disney version – a nice guy with good intentions gets eaten by the big bad wolf." He stood and offered his hand. "I hope you do the right thing. Think about it."

Spenser heard the car drive away, yet still he sat. Trash

bags waited by the door. If he left them overnight the mice would feast. There would be a mess in the morning. Mice inside, raccoons outside. He'd have to haul them down to the dumpster by the barracks before dark. But for now he could only sit and seethe. The Disney version.

In bed he stared at the ceiling. He couldn't sleep. He got up and paced the building. He was right, damn it. Chandler had been buried alive by a self-serving army establishment. He and all he stood for damn well deserved a champion. Of course the establishment would try to discredit any effort to rehabilitate him. Of course Spenser, as his flag bearer, would be tested. That was the price he had to pay for doing the right thing.

All those pleased veterans this afternoon, the great feedback. It was the confirmation he had been craving, and it was proof, damn it – proof that he had made a powerful case and the people who mattered most were behind him. Their grievances were aired – finally! The evidence was behind glass for all to see. Damned if he'd back down now.

And yet, and yet: The Disney version. The words hounded him. But then look at the price Chandler paid for sticking to his convictions. He'd just have to take the heat – from the army, from the academics, even a few disgruntled vets – as long as he stayed true to what he and Chandler stood for. The guys who mattered – most of them, at least – were with him. The open house was proof of that. Stick to your guns.

And yet...

He woke to a room filled with sunshine. It was the morning of the day after, and, damn it, he was happy.

Unburdened. His big day was history, and it was a triumph, naysayers be damned. The gods had awarded him another gorgeous summer day, but when a cloud of dust rose over the window sill he tossed off the sheet and stood for a better view. Someone was heading up the driveway in another colorless little sedan. Or was it Benbow again? Why? Had he been pacing and ruminating, too?

At the sink he splashed his face, gargled and spat. He yanked on yesterday's sweaty pants and shirt. He was tying his shoes when the hollow sound of footsteps on the porch reached him. Let him wait, damn it. Let him fume. The guy tried the door, then knocked. Well, fuck him. If he wanted a fight, he'd get one. John resolved to speak first. This time he'd take the offensive

He yanked the door open upon two smiling faces. Flight suits. Garrison caps bearing bright silver stars. They were Air Guard generals, sleek, boyish, and to the cockpit born. Bright and early on this beautiful morning, two generals stood in the doorway beaming at him.

The brigadier offered his hand. "Good morning, John Spenser! Can we talk?"

Good news travels fast. They must have heard what a success the open house was – right here in the old club where they had partied as young lieutenants.

"Of course, General. A little early for a tour, but I'm up for it if you are."

"Another time, for sure. Our public affairs shop briefed us on what a magnificent job you've done here, Spenser. It's gratifying to know that our old club is in your hands and that it has been serving such a worthy cause.

But frankly we're here on an altogether different matter. It's a long story. Maybe we should sit."

They sat. The major general took over: The air force had long been concerned that its training program did not adequately address the variety of combat scenarios it was likely to encounter in a complex air-ground European environment, and this was especially true for reserve components like the Air National Guard. Modern technology, however, was creating a whole new ballgame...

Spenser had gone to bed stuffed with Spam and eggs. He woke up craving sweets. He lost the thread of the generals' tag team presentation wondering if, by chance, they had left a sack of donuts in the car. His first foolish assumption was that they had come to congratulate him. Now he knew better. Wherever this filibuster was headed, it meant trouble. Why else would the two of them so unctuously belabor him with their problems?

...Out of all the states competing for the honor, all with first-class reserve components and high quality locations, only five would be selected by the Pentagon to accommodate these remarkable, next generation facilities. At a news conference yesterday the Secretary of Defense named the winners, and by god, top of the list was the Camp Palmer Air National Guard component...

"Now hear me out, John. We are talking about a vote of confidence from Uncle Sam in the tens of millions, and we are one hundred percent dedicated to shepherding this project to a successful completion in record time... Aircraft from installations throughout the Midwest, from old B-52s and A-10s right up to stealth fighters still on the drawing boards will fly combat scenarios over our heads and beyond... wide-ranging, free play combat exercises over terrain that is a virtual analogue of its central European counterpart... microwave stations scattered over a dozen counties will record every move... and the beating heart of the whole operation will be the radar complex to be sited right where we sit today... Old Camp Palmer, birthplace of the state militia, will become the nerve center of a new age Air Combat Maneuvering Instrumentation System..."

In other words, Old Camp Palmer as Spenser knew it was to be displaced by a vast underground bunker with an overlaying behemoth of brick and steel encapsulating a queen bee supercomputer which would rule over a statewide network of slave subordinates. Spenser recalled the surveyors in orange vests and tin hats. Now he understood.

They were sitting at a table, each with a paper cup of water that, like the colonel yesterday, they rotated with their fingers but did not drink from.

"A computer game," Spenser said. "You're kicking us out for a computer game."

They glanced at each other and smiled. "Get used to it, friend," the brigadier said. "Remember, there will be only five such installations in the whole country. We are destined to host a training tool so advanced over anything our potential adversaries..."

He was pathetically overmatched. Two generals, tens of millions of dollars. No wonder they were so chummy. They were trying to break his fall even as they kicked his legs out from under him. He reminded himself that flight suits were no big deal. Guys washed the dog and took out the trash in their precious flight suits. He would not be swaddled and rocked. He had a museum to protect, and he would not be scared off by a couple of fast-talkers in flight suits – even flight suits bearing stars.

"Now as to this impressive collection of artifacts you have on display here, John, we know full well its significance for you Bold Eagle folks. But today the hammer has fallen. Change is a'comin' to Old Camp Palmer. It's rolling down the track big time, but I promise you that we on the air side hold our Bold Eagle heritage as dear as you on the ground side. Air is sworn to work hand in hand with ground to relocate you to a facility within the New Camp cantonment area. That building *will* be upgraded to professional standards as budgets permit over the coming years..."

He got the message. They weren't saving the museum. They were burying it. They didn't give a damn about the museum. Uncle Sam had just made them rich, famous and promotable. They were on a sugar high. The museum would be tucked away in one faded grey barracks among hundreds of faded grey clones. It would be a museum without visitors. Outsiders would go crazy looking for it. A museum in New Camp would be a ghost museum in a ghost town, and his own revisionist history of the neglected Bold Eagle division would become that sound in the forest that no one hears.

Again his visitors exchanged glances. The baton went back to the major general: "I promise you right here and now that you will be retained at your current GS pay grade though with a necessarily modified position description. While your collections are being stored pending facility upgrades, you will be getting the paperwork side up and running, classifying acquisitions and whatnot. Now John, we've been led to believe that you are counting down after a splendid career in army intel. Tell me how long you have left. Three years? Four?"

Such an innocent question. Such a diabolical man. The general was ready to deal. Spenser understood his choices. He could either surrender his sword or suffer the consequences. A curator determined to liberate the Bold Eagle division and its rightful commander from the army's self-serving narrative of the Ponga campaign would stand his ground come what may. A curator who was convinced that the regular army had made whipping boys of a National Guard infantry division and its leader in order to cover the ass of a celebrity five-star – the very drama queen who had recklessly sent them into the jungle unprepared and fatally misinformed – would not be bought off with reassuring chitchat about retirement. He would go down fighting. Was Spenser that dedicated curator, or did he just need a few more years until his pension kicked in? That's what the general really wanted to know. The bullet-headed son of a bitch knew what he was doing.

Spenser held out, stewing, but he knew where this was headed. "About three," he said.

"Not a problem," the general said, nodding sagely. "Three is doable. With dandy quarters in an upgraded BOQ, mess privileges and whatnot, you'll live a lot higher on the hog than what you got here. Now then, we'll assign airmen to assist you in packing up and moving out as soon as the army side frees up a building. Everything you got here – the glass cases, the artifacts, the whole shebang – has got to go."

1989

———

Someone rapped on the window. Hagan woke to a light in his eyes. He was parked behind a fancy sign of some sort. He had lost his sense of direction and needed time to get his head straight. That's all he remembered.

"Can't park here. Private property," the man said.

Hagan lowered his window. The guy was an officer of some kind. "I got off the interstate and got lost," Hagan told him. "I guess I fell asleep."

The light was lowered and the man leaned closer to the window. "Been drinking, friend?"

"No."

"Not a good time of day for old-timers like you and me to go exploring. Where you headed?"

"I'm not sure. Mostly I just wanted a place to catch my breath."

"You sure you haven't been drinking?"

"Give me the damn test. I'll prove it."

The flashlight went out. "Got family nearby? Someone I could call?"

"I don't need to be rescued. I just need to sit for a spell. A roadmap would help if you have one."

"I don't carry maps. I'm private security. Somehow you wandered into the Duffydale Estates."

"Is there a motel nearby?"

"Yeah, not far, but not a straight shot either. A lot of curvy roads between here and the well-lit world."

"So where is this Duffydale?"

"All around you, through the trees, up the winding drives. Mostly well-off seniors who are smart enough not to go wandering around in the dark. Unlike you and me."

Hagan took comfort. He got the message. The man didn't want a confrontation. "I guess we'd both rather be somewhere else," he ventured. "I take it you'd rather be at the dinner table. Why aren't you, if you don't mind?"

"Oh, the usual. Bad attitude and dumb choices early in life," the man said. "Need the income. And yourself?"

Hagan was beginning to feel at home with this chap. "My dining table is half a world away. Weather permitting, it would be on the patio of our house on Hilda Street in Balwin, a lovely suburb of Melbourne, Australia. I have been missing that house and that patio very much lately. But I grew up in Drumlin, so I come back now and then."

"Face it, friend, you're lost. You're not the first to flee the highway and wind up in Duffydale. Traffic on the big road won't thin out till the wee hours, a long wait for a big fella in a small car. I've got a better way for you to spend your time. How about you follow me down the road a bit?"

Hagan was in a mood for solitude, but what the hell? With any luck there would be a bathroom.

He fell in behind the officer's jeep. The guy was right about the curvy roads. What little Hagan could glimpse of meandering houses shrouded in hanging foliage reminded him of that fateful post-war visit to Drumlin to work out a deal with his ex, when he ended up spending the night in jail. To work up his courage that day he had driven around town only to discover a new neighborhood of earth-hugging 'ranches' of stone and plate glass with pastel Chryslers and Packards glistening in driveways like tropical plants, and once again he had felt excluded as he had in high school. Oh the lure of wealth, leisure, and sex. Damned if he was going to stay on the outside looking in forever.

In the darkness of an autumn night in Duffydale nearly half a century later he cruised a twin of that neighborhood. Away from the streetlights' flattering glow, the trees and shrubbery had turned menacing, bullying everything in their path. Sidewalks were upended, curbs and corners obscured, rooftops smothered. Fragile mid-century saplings had morphed into monsters that swarmed and heaved and suffocated. Thank God for the jeep's tail-lights rising and dipping and easing around curves ahead, guiding him through the forest.

They negotiated a steep driveway made hazardous by washouts. At the top of the hill Hagan pulled in beside the jeep at a sprawling adobe-like enclosure. He followed the officer down a stairway beside the adobe wall, ducking wet branches much of the way. The building seemed to be a sort of hacienda layered into the side of a hill on a series of terraces. The plate-glass windows of all four stories lit up a valley steaming with flora. It was like a piece of New Mexico sunk deep into a northwoods hillside, a triumph of imagination over reality.

At the bottom floor the officer rapped on a window frame. The glass door slid open. A sallow face appeared. Thick glasses, slicked white hair, a hail fellow grin. "So, Walter, you bagged another one." He was almost yelling, as though to speak over his headphones.

"You got it, Mr Duffy. Another wanderer." The officer stepped aside to make room for Hagan, whose hand was snatched into a two-fisted squeeze. "A lost soul!" Duffy shouted. "Come in, friend! *Mi casa es su casa!*"

Hagan reclaimed his hand. "I'm not really lost. I just have to find my way back to the interstate."

Duffy pointed at the earphones. "You have to speak up! My daily period of spiritual renewal!"

Hagan said, "I'd like to use your bathroom!"

Duffy pointed. "Down the hall! Then keep going to the kitchen. Juanita will know what to do!"

It was a long hallway. Hagan tried to imagine how much of the hill had to be hauled away to make room for this place.

The door was open. The light was on. He closed the door behind him. He felt too shaky to stand, so he dropped his pants. Sitting there, still trembling, he shut his eyes. He pictured himself on his back under a giant rainbow umbrella. Music came from somewhere. The smell of coconut oil was in the air. Sleek, sweat-beaded backs and butts sprawled all around him. A fruity gin drink was in his hand. His bladder emptied. Mellowness enveloped him.

He opened his eyes upon a desiccated night crawler stuck to the white tile floor. Where it had come from and where was it going?

In the kitchen an old woman with a brightly colored shawl over her shoulders said, "Sit please. *Uno momento*."

She brought coffee and a plate of bacon and eggs. Spreading out from the base of the ceiling light, he noticed, were networks of very fine cracks. It occurred to him that up close, maybe they weren't so fine. He happened to look up because something seemed to be drifting down upon his eggs. It was so infinitely small that he didn't exactly see it but sensed it.

It was a relief to head back to the front room with its windows onto the world and a handy exit, but he'd have to deal with that Duffy fellow. He wanted to be away and alone. A decision had to be made. Was he headed to O'Hare or not? Was he heading home or back to Old Camp?

Duffy was relaxing at his desk, that vivacious smile frozen in place rictus-like. The headphones were around his neck for now. As Hagan approached, he spoke up, calm and welcoming: "Turn around, my friend. Take a gander at that wall. My grandfather. His story. Duffydale wouldn't exist without him. More importantly, Motivation Unlimited – The Duffy System, wouldn't exist. It all began with him."

The room was enormous. The wall Duffy referred to was in shadow except for overhead lamps illuminating a mural. On the far left a scowling young man in a collarless shirt, sleeves rolled, stood on a bleak stretch of prairie beside a contraption that might have been a medieval torture device on wheels. 'Our First Twine Binder', said the brass plate. The image faded into another scene in which the head and shoulders of an older man drifted over factory buildings and more red machines – tractors, harvesters, wheeled haulers. In the final scene a stern, ghostly visage in the clouds keeps watch over an industrial metropolis. The brass plate said, 'Progress, Pride, Perseverance'.

Duffy's jaw hung slack. On his desk was an open attaché case lined in purple velveteen. Plastic cassettes bearing inscriptions in gold were fitted into the lining.

"Ever hear of the Duffy System?" Duffy asked.

"I'm afraid not," Hagan said.

"Motivation Unlimited?"

"No, sorry to say."

"Make yourself comfortable on the sofa over there. You must be tired. Stretch out if you like. I won't be offended. Fall asleep? That's fine too. Long story. It will soak in either way. Every day since college I have listened to one complete lesson. Every day, faithfully. It has become the most restful, fulfilling and blessed hour of my day."

Reluctantly, Hagan did as he was told. He was a guest after all, and he had been generously treated. The sofa was very comfortable. Lying there, he noticed something about that wall that he had not been aware of before. All along the intersection of ceiling and wall, just above the light fixtures, was a fringe of dead vegetation – no blossoms, no greenery, just bushy, bristly fiber, or so it appeared from his angle.

A voice rich with good fellowship burst over him: "We are off on a journey together, you and I. Our train speeds deep into the night passing vast fields starved of rain, past towns sinking into dust and debt, a world of pain and hunger and despair, yet you must succeed for the survival of your firm – even your measure as a man – will depend upon the outcome of this venture. You see reflected in the window a face furrowed with fear and uncertainty. Fear that you will fall short, that you are not equal to the vast, suffering marketplace before you... Welcome, friend, to lesson one, Motivation Unlimited – The Duffy System... "

He woke with a gritty tongue. He took out his handkerchief and tried to spit but couldn't. Something was drifting down. It was grittier than smoke but almost invisible. The back of his forearm was furry with the stuff.

He noticed that Duffy had draped a towel over his head, and when he took it off and swatted it against his knee, a cloud of dust hung in the air. "Not to worry," Duffy said. "No big deal. The house is still settling in. Still shedding debris from time to time."

Hagan took a second look at that fibrous growth above the mural. No wonder there were no leaves or blossoms. No wonder it was earth colored. It was a mass of feelers from a mighty root system, most likely the looming giants he had passed under coming down the stairway. Trees were gnawing into the very guts of the house.

Somewhere overhead a woman was making a fuss. Was there a Mrs Duffy? Did she too wake up with a mouth full of dirt?

"You ask, why replicate here in the muggy, mildewy Midwest, on a hillside no less, a piece of the sun-baked south-west?" Duffy said. "Because my father learned from his father that if you've got the spunk, the spirit, the can-do frame of mind, you *can* do anything, that's why! And *that* is heart and soul of Motivation Unlimited – the Duffy System. It motivated millions through the darkness of the Depression, the horrors of war, and brought about the wealth of mid-century blessings that at long last allowed my father to convert his treasured dream of Duffydale into a reality.

"Our light has dimmed in these crazy times, my friend, but I keep the faith, and you can too, Mr..."

"Hagan. Jack Hagan."

"Yes. You too can catch the flame and keep it alive through daily immersion into the Duffy System via these treasured tapes that I am giving you today, free gratis, the whole system as laid out by my grandfather over half a century ago and later brought to perfection by my father during those golden post-war years of growth and power and joy."

The words came from his mouth but might as well have been on tape, so automated did he seem with that fixed grin and rat-a-tat delivery. 'Eyes on the prize... nose to the grindstone... Mind your P's and Q's...'

Jack smelled the drifting dirt. He sat and brushed it from his hair. He felt like he was suffocating. What was wrong with him? Why was he sitting still for this nonsense? Everywhere, people had been hiding away from him or taking vengeance on him. Now here he sat, immobilzed by a high priest of hucksterism. He'd come all this way to make peace only to be met with coldness, rejection, and harangues. Wake up you fool! You don't belong here! Not in Duffydale, not in this crazy country, not anymore.

And what about poor Johnny? Was this the world he'd grown up in? The image of a store sign flashed in his head: *Hagan and Son Florists*. It couldn't happen, of course. Far too late for that, but the '*and son*' hit home. Maybe this long ordeal he'd put himself through was going to pay off after all – as a rescue mission. What a life the poor kid could make for himself in Australia – free from the bitter household he'd grown up in and the crazy pressure thereafter to succeed or die of shame. Melbourne could be his liberation, his last chance to become a complete man.

"... Embrace the program. Live the program, and you will wander no more, my friend. You will know where you're going, you will know when you get there, and you will be a fulfilled man."

"Very nice of you, Mr Duffy," Hagan said, getting to his feet, "but you must understand I'm traveling light and I am overdue. Many thanks for the delightful supper and many comforts, but I'm afraid..."

"Oh, I understand. We shy away from what's good for us. We don't trust it, and it scares us. That's human nature. So just take one of our little briefcases with you. It is designed for travel and comes complete with all twelve lessons and a player, batteries and headphones included. Listen while you drive, share the Duffy System with your friends. Remember the name: Motivation Unlimited – the Duffy System. Let's bring it back to life, you and me. The world needs it now more than ever."

Hagan had his eye on that sliding glass door. "Very much obliged, Mr Duffy. Now if I may..."

He was not built for a fast getaway, especially up flights of stairs, and at the top he gasped and his vision went dim, his legs wobbly again, but the car was right where he'd left it, and the keys were in his hand.

Memorial

"**I**T'LL BE A GREAT DAY," SPENSER ASSURED HIS MOTHER on their way to the new mall outside of town. "No big deal, just a brief ceremony. A few VIPs will mumble platitudes. Some old-timers are bound to show up. Their wives will probably bring food. It would be great if you'd come along and see what I was up to."

She gazed at the passing fields, pondering. "Oh John, I don't think so. It's so far and I don't want to miss my four o'clock meds. Take pictures and tell me about it later."

The dedication ceremony at Old Camp was being held the next day. The statue of Sergeant High and Private Low was being officially unveiled. Of all Spenser's visions for the Bold Eagle museum, this was the sole survivor.

He didn't press her. Her response was about what he had expected. He had done his duty. Case closed.

She had other things on her mind, the house in particular. "Nothing wastes away like an empty house," she often reminded him.

His mother had been on his mind ever since he settled

into his apartment in the Bachelor Officers' Quarters at New Camp Palmer. The building had recently been gutted, insulated, rewired and updated to accommodate people year-round. New appliances, his own bathroom, a view from the tiny kitchen of wooded hills where, in season, the rituals of tank gunnery and small unit tactical exercises were played out, though by now the summer soldiers were long gone. Only a few guard and reserve officers had shared the building with him, short course types who came and went before he even learned their names.

It had taken him weeks to come to terms with his new reality – the pending destruction of the Lodge and conversion of Old Camp into a digital wonder world – and thus the end of the Bold Eagle museum as he had envisioned it. And it had taken him that long to admit that there was a silver lining. A load had been lifted. The museum would have been a work in progress forever, a constant drain on his resolve and stamina. But a museum in storage was another matter altogether. No one would see it. No one would criticize. And as for the deal he had settled for, well, damn it, it was pretty generous. They say you can't live in the past, but Spenser had been guaranteed three more years to do just that – at his current salary and in subsidized comfort. His artifacts and exhibits were already stashed in another barracks nearby in New Camp where he had created his own little make-do office with heat and light and work space and above all, privacy. He had books to read and plenty of the war in the Pacific yet to follow the Bold Eagle division through. Three years to be as busy and immersed in the past as he wanted to be. It was almost shameful how quickly he had accommodated himself to this downgraded version of his mission – a comfy, well-subsidized three-year sabbatical with a pension to follow.

All of which had brought to mind his mother. He had been remiss. Months had gone by. In her last call she had reminded him that winter wasn't far off. Should the dehumidifier be shut down or was it too early? Furnace filters had to be replaced before the heating season. Mold, mildew, insects, rodents, dust and grime. Who knew what was gnawing away at the place? Such a grand and needy old property. Such out of control hedges and lilacs and trees. So much to check on and keep up with and fix.

She used a wheelchair now, and a good thing too because they had to cross a desert of baking asphalt and gleaming auto roofs to get into the mall. At the Pendleton shop his mother found a sweater she liked. Her original plan was to come up with a peace offering for her lifelong pal Tillie, but Tillie had backed out at the last minute and so she picked out a cardigan for herself, navy and white stripes with mother of pearl buttons.

Ruminating aloud during the drive back to Drumlin, the sweater in a bag on her lap, she confessed that she'd taken Tillie for granted, expecting her to pick up dry cleaning, help with insurance paperwork she'd put off – too many errands and in return, too little gratitude and compassion for an old friend. Spenser knew what was behind the self-criticism. Whenever that old cloud of peevishness and spite settled over his mother for weeks on end she bit every hand extended to her. Through the years she had driven away almost everyone who'd ever been close. A lingering sense of grievance had dimmed everything, and not much was left of the lively, cute-as-a-button high school prodigy who, she'd boasted then, would be the university's first woman graduate in the mechanical engineering school, following in her father's footsteps.

But even before she got to college things had gone haywire. Terrible headlines, doomsday threats from both sides of the world, old classmates returning home in uniform, the thrill of being sucked into the vortex of great events, life-changing decisions made on the spur of the moment. Maybe she never really had a shot at engineering school anyway. Maybe deep down she didn't really want to be an engineer. She would never know for sure because she got pregnant and abandoned and spent her life as a library assistant in the old Carnegie building.

Ever since, the worst part of her day was late afternoon when coppery sunlight glared on upper stories but cast the world below into shadow. Back home she'd lie on the living room sofa muttering to the ceiling about lingering hurts from the past, a long-dead teacher's remark about her bobbed hair, a sense of being pushed into things before she was ready, reviewing all the things that had gone wrong. During the war they had lived in a rush of urgent stories that might have explained certain disappearances and an empty mailbox, and she'd come to conclusions about people she didn't hear from anymore. Her misfortunes were related to the war. She'd been a casualty of sorts. Meanwhile her father prowled the halls and hid out in his basement workshop, and her mother tended her tulips and zinnias and wished she could talk to her daughter about the mid-day agricultural interviews on the radio, the bee keepers and dog breeders and soil scientists, the folks who brought to mind the old spring lists and the possibility of embarking on new projects. She craved conversation. She tried to help her daughter become good company again, to nurse her back into a world of cheerful awareness and brisk conversation. That was the saving grace. Good company was all there was left to be. Lively conversation is what she tried to launch at the supper table night after night against the forces of indifference, distraction, and loss of pep. Sometimes that's how supper turned out. The smell of meat loaf or boiled dinner, the clink and clatter of desultory dining, and at last a heartening but one-sided burst of chatter from Grandma.

Meanwhile a man droning the Chicago grain and livestock reports was their cue that soon the exalted voice of the nightly news would burst over them. It was that voice that had carried them through the dark years of good versus evil. But his mother had already given up. She knew the news she had been waiting for would never come. The voice went on, year after year, through Korea and the Cold War, Vietnam, the death of John's grandfather and his grandmother's last years at the retirement home.

So there would be no Tillie to lighten the mood this afternoon. There had been so many late-season cook-outs through the years but fewer and fewer people to enliven them, and today it would be just the two of them. He was already dreading it.

She was right about the house. It was stuffy. Windows had to be opened right away, upstairs and down, but by late afternoon he had the satisfaction of watching carbonized debris of sirloins past sizzle to life, writhe in the heat waves and drift away from the grill he had set up in the backyard. An abandoned wasp nest went up like a tropical hootch in a newsreel. He had spread an old sheet on the bench of the picnic table and helped his mother transfer from the wheelchair to a corner seat. She ignored the brandy old-fashioned he had fixed for her. What haunted them both, he knew, were the voices that were missing, their original neighbors, her father's work friends and their wives, even her closest friends from school. There's nothing so melancholy as a family tradition on life support.

A while later, smoke rising from under the dome stirred his blood. A big slab of sirloin was charring over the coals as in days of old, and just then came the unexpected sound of a vehicle crunching up the gravel drive. Good old Tillie had changed her mind.

"There you are, old dear!" she cried, wobbling around the side of the house. "Oh Johnny, it smells heavenly. Hello! Hello!"

If that was liquid courage speaking, who could blame her? She leaned over to plant a big wet kiss on his mother's cheek. "I didn't know if you really wanted me here, Sukie, but I decided, oh the hell with it, I want to be with my old pal!" Sukie. That's what they called each other. It went back forever. John was heartened by the sight of them together again, the awkward hug, the teary eyes and cheerful nonsense.

"I'm so happy you came," his mother said. "I know I've been a big poop lately."

"Well, you've been blue. I understand. We all have our moments."

Spenser headed to the kitchen. "I'll get you something to drink."

"Whatever you two are drinking, Johnny. Looks good to me."

From the kitchen window he watched them chatter away, heads bowed like co-conspirators. He'd always loved Tillie's air of breezy obliviousness. She had the high-shouldered, high-chinned self-regard of a forties' starlet, and like them she smoked with a flippant sort of elegance, as though the payoff was in the performance – lighting up, spurting smoke at the sky, mercilessly crushing the embers. She brought his mother to life in a way that no one else could. Tillie's lifelong grievance was that she'd never been able to shake Harry, the guy who had staked his claim in high school and followed her to college, sealing her away from more promising candidates, but Harry was long gone and she'd become a liberated, caffeinated, high-energy widow.

Spenser was relieved to be out of the picture for now. The water softener needed a bag of salt, and there were furnace filters to deal with. The rest would have to wait.

"Belle of the ball!" Tillie was saying as he hurried back to the Weber. "And you knew it! Yes you did! Such great times and such wonderful fellas. Little did anyone know..." As he lifted the dome a plume of smoke swept over the table, shocking Tillie back to the present. "We're talking about Louisiana, Johnny. The spring of forty-two before the boys shipped out. Those were the days."

Clouds had moved in, and a breeze chilled the sweat on his neck. For a moment fall was in the air. The steak was perfect. While he and Tillie dug in, his mother chewed a few bits he'd cut up for her but mostly she just pushed them around and nibbled her salad.

"So for me, Louisiana meant Free at last! Free at last!" Tillie went on. "At least for those two weeks." She sighed. "Didn't we surprise ourselves, though?"

Later he walked her to her car, holding her arm. "I hope I didn't get out of line," she said. "Once I get yapping I never know."

"You were great. You made the day for us, but why don't you let me drive you home?"

"Don't be ridiculous." Like his mother's Oldsmobile, her car was a red sedan from the era of swaggering hulks, and when she pulled on the door it lunged at her, throwing her off balance. She dug through her bag for the keys. She had teared up and was clearly flustered.

"Tillie, it was a great afternoon. Really." Just then he remembered the sweater. "In fact she brought you a gift. I almost forgot. Hang on. I'll run back and get it."

"No, Johnny, don't. Let her think about it. She can call me tomorrow if she wants, and I'll drop by her place to pick it up. She might have second thoughts. You know how she gets."

"I hate to see you go off like this. You two were having a great time."

Tillie was not so sure. "I thought she ought to show some interest in what you've been doing up there at Camp Palmer. She told me about tomorrow, and I went and opened my big mouth, and now I'm afraid I may have messed up your big day."

When he got back to his mother she was hugging herself. "I'm ready to go," she said. "Suddenly it's chilly."

On the drive to the manor she told him she had changed her mind about tomorrow. She wanted to be with him when the statue was unveiled.

* * *

They emerged from the woods and headed along the dirt road to the grassy basin of Old Camp. "That's it, Mom," he said. "Up the side of the hill. That's Building One, the Lodge, where it all began. Hallowed ground. I thought it was torn down weeks ago. I'll give you a tour after the ceremony."

It was one of those energizing fall days, bright, brisk, startlingly clear and splashed with color. His mother had caught the spirit, dressing in autumnal plaids and smart shoes, and best of all she'd been downright chatty during the long ride up, going on about good times for a change, a hay ride with high school pals, fall auto trips with her parents to see the colors.

Earth-moving machines were lined side by side on the field below the Lodge – bulldozers and a couple dump trucks. Where the brick barracks once stood there was a gaping hole set off by snow fencing and caution tape. "The Lodge will be torn down soon," he told her. "Enormous antennas will go up there. A brick and cement blockhouse stuffed with computers is being built where the barracks used to be. By next summer, Old Camp as the vets knew it will be gone."

But today was all about the debut of Spenser's two terrified but resolute riflemen, Sergeant High and Private Low. They were destined to become the only reminder of what Old Camp was originally all about. By this time next year they would be creeping up on the world's most elaborate computer game.

Cars were parked in the field within easy walking distance of the draped statue. Portapotties had been set up well apart from tables of barbecued meatballs, pasta salad, and sheet cake where the ladies had gathered. Groups of old guys in sweatshirts and Bold Eagle baseball caps killed time together. Spenser recognized some faces. He was pleased to see the board of trustees well represented.

He parked in the grassy triangle that separated the dirt road and the lane uphill to the Lodge. It was as close to midway between the Lodge and the statue as he could get. While lifting his mother's collapsed wheelchair from the back of the truck he sized up the crowd. Maybe forty or fifty veterans and a couple dozen wives. A decent turnout. He would have been intimidated by a bigger crowd, disappointed by a smaller one. The hum of chatter was punctuated by occasional bursts of laughter. He was struck by the neighborly feel of this gathering. The breeze smelled of wide open spaces and barbecue sauce.

A podium, a microphone, the tarpaulin-draped figures, but as yet no VIPs. It wasn't hard to imagine those old guys crowded into a latrine half a century ago, lathering up, staring at the steel mirrors and wondering what continent they would wake up on next month. How many of the original group were too feeble to show up, too oblivious to care, or long departed?

"It's so beautiful here," his mother said as he swung her into the chair. "I've never been to this part of the state. The hills, that great big meadow, bluffs like out west, and it's so hidden away." He tilted the chair back and eased her off the turf and onto the road. Up ahead, a couple yards from the podium loomed the draped form. As he pushed her in that direction a few old-timers waved hello. "There he is," one of them said, "the man of the hour."

As they approached the podium he backed her chair off the road and into the crowd. "Can you handle the bumps?" he asked.

"Aren't we close enough already? Where are you supposed to be?"

"I guess this is as good a place as any."

He wondered how many old-timers were not happy to see him. The museum he had been hired to bring to life had instead been relegated to a sort of time capsule. In spite of assurances from the Air Guard generals, the odds that it would ever be resurrected were dim given the shrinking pool of veterans pushing for it. It wasn't his fault, but he had been the captain when the ship went down.

Some clean-shaven, shiny-faced old guys beside them were having a serious chat. It seemed someone they expected had not shown up, and they had just learned why. Spenser heard language that would never have been spoken by their young soldier selves: "A beautiful man... A sweetheart of a guy...," and he realized that for them this little get-together was more than a dedication ceremony. It was as though they had toured many sites, endured many trials, and seen many relics together, and today's unveiling could not distract them from the news that really mattered.

A deep roll of thunder came out of the sky. Eyes turned to the western bluff where a diamond-shaped formation of fighter jets came swooping over the horizon of pines.

Heads ducked and swivelled east, watching the planes disappear. His mother remained stooped until the sound faded. If he'd known, he would have warned her. Finally she looked around for him, her face pale and maybe a little indignant. But seeing him she managed a smile. Figures had appeared on the podium, and a voice over the loudspeaker urged "A big cheer for the sound of freedom!"

The speaker, a hardy old-timer in a Bold Eagle baseball cap and a T-shirt that said, *Here today, Gone to Maui,* put his hand over his heart. "Welcome one and all. Will you please join me..."

After a scratchy recording of the national anthem an Air Guard chaplain offered a prayer, and an army officer took over the microphone to extol the Bold Eagle division and all it had accomplished throughout the long struggle to bring peace, prosperity and democracy to distant lands on the far side of the globe.

John had a hard time making sense of what came out of the terrible sound system. Probably everyone did. And probably it didn't matter. It was what you put up with on such occasions. What mattered was that it wouldn't last long, and that when it ended, onlookers could all go back to their private conversations.

A list of names was being read. He made out his own. There was a splatter of applause, and finally the tarpaulin slid away revealing his creation rendered in swampish greens and earthen browns. Sergeant High and Private Low were life-sized as he had imagined them but elevated on a pedestal. In a more realistic depiction they would have hugged the ground, but elevation gave them a certain dignity, something never granted the fighters they stood for by the army in its version of the story. That was fine with John. They deserved to be looked up to for a change. Even here in peaceful, sunny, decommissioned Old Camp, where the deer and the chipmunks browsed, where snow would blanket them and ice would hang from their sweaty faces, they stalked and lunged. To Spenser there was something suspiciously resin-like about the surface. He wondered if over time the colors would fade and the savagery of the image would give way to a fiberglass shell over a network of plastic pipes. But no, he wouldn't go there. He refused to worry. For now he was pleased. It was a job well done.

The crowd seemed to agree. Among the women he noticed hands pressed to lips and maybe even some tears.

There were handshakes and pats on the back, but not much was said, and gradually people drifted back to the food tables and into small groups, until only Spenser and his mother were looking on.

"It's very striking," she said finally. "I don't know what to say." Spenser would have spent more time with his two old friends, studying them from different angles, letting the experience sink in, but he knew she was getting antsy.

"I'll need to get to a bathroom soon, John, and I don't mean those rent-a-potty things."

He had expected this. By the time he had backed her wheelchair onto the road, vehicles were already pulling out and heading back to the real world. As he had anticipated, the unveiling had turned out to be no big deal. A few minutes out of a Sunday afternoon, a brief distraction from family and chores. So who else would ever set eyes on those struggling warriors? Workers heading to and from their terminals at the computer installation would soon weary of them. Visitors taking a break from the interstate might picnic in their shadow. A few families might show up to pay respects to Grandpa's war – what little they understood of it. But year round, season after season, Sergeant High and Private Low's most constant companions were likely to be circling hawks, grazing deer, and other meadow critters.

He U-turned his mother's chair onto the driveway and bent to the task. It was a long haul to the Lodge, but he welcomed the chance to burn off pent-up energy. At the foot of the porch steps he said, "Hang on!" and turned the chair around again, making her the caboose as he tilted it backwards and pulled it – thump, thump – up to the porch. Reaching into his pocket for keys he glanced again at the departing vehicles and was surprised to see a car slowly advancing against the outward flow. Why would anyone show up now? Even at a distance the car looked familiar. It was another putty-colored sedan like the one Colonel Disney Version had driven off in.

He unlocked the door. It opened upon a cavernous

emptiness. "This is it, Mom. You're entering living history."

Gallery One was hardly recognizable. The fleshy bar was missing. So too the smoky mirror, dangling jets, and display cases. Only the lingering stink of good times gone stale remained.

He pushed her chair into the cool cave that was Gallery Two. "The place is so much bigger than it looked from the outside," his mother said. "It reminds me of the old dance pavilion at Lake Sophie."

The bathroom was in Gallery Three. The door stood open. Though she was unsteady on her feet she insisted she could manage, and so he retreated to the kitchen, his former office and bedroom, and stood at the window. The new arrival was heading up the driveway. Had he locked the front door? No, it stood open.

His mother called. He found her back in the wheelchair, waiting. "Someone's coming," he told her. "I have my suspicions. I don't want to see him. We'll wait this out in my old room."

He hurried her into the kitchen and locked the door behind them. "You lived here?" she said, taking in the stained ceiling, hanging conduit and other evidence that his home for months had been an abandoned greasy spoon.

"Yes, but we have to be quiet now. I don't want the guy to know I'm here."

"Jack, what's going on?"

Again he went to the window but peered cautiously to avoid being seen. His right hand sought out the medallion in his pants pocket. It was a miniature of the one the veterans had presented to General Chandler and which had ended up in a place of honor on his patio. Spenser knew he had no right to it. He also knew he would never part with it. From the moment he discovered it in a pocket of a deceased major's dress blues he had resolved to keep it. It had been intended for him. That's how he felt. It was his personal link to Graham Chandler and all that he stood for.

"I don't want to see the guy, that's all. Our business is over and done with. He's getting out of the car."

"Well go tell him that, why don't you?"

"Shush, please! This has been a great day. I don't want it to end with an argument."

Her face had that old familiar look. Storm warning. Whatever the hell was going on she didn't like it one bit. If she made a scene...

Footsteps echoed from the porch. Okay, Spenser thought, check the place out, take a look around and go away. No one's home. Nothing to see, nothing to talk about.

More footsteps. The guy was in Gallery One, muttering to himself.

He advanced slowly, as though disoriented. Was something missing? Had he expected display cases, maps and battle scenes only to find himself adrift in space?

Whatever was going on in his head, he was getting closer. A shadow moved across the window of the door, and there was a light tap on the glass, as though by a timid fingertip. But there was nothing timid about the two angry knocks that followed. Spenser sucked air and held it. He turned a shoulder to the door to brace himself should it come crashing open, relaxing only when the steps moved away, fading towards Gallery Three.

A few moments later, an outburst: "Some museum you got here, Johnny, me boy! Bare walls and a great gloomy emptiness. I've come a helluva long ways. An explanation is in order, if you please. We've got a lot to talk about, you and me. So much to say, so little time."

* * *

By God, he made it. For all the fucking distractions and bullshit obstacles fate and his own creepy impulses had put in his way, from midnight bouts of dread and crumbling resolve to poor, sick Vivian in the back seat, he had persevered. He made it. He was back at Old Camp Palmer.

A glance in the rear-view mirror reminded Hagan what a sleazebag he'd become – greasy hair, greasy stubble, greasy bags under his eyes. He stank and the car was a mess. Avis would be unhappy with him. Did O'Hare have showers? Would he have to wait until tomorrow for a flight? He vowed to be clean-shaven and decent-smelling when he boarded the plane. He wanted his daughters to rush him and hug him and flood him with all the love and regard that had been denied him 'back home'.

But one hurdle remained, the whole reason for this fiasco. Yes, he'd taken a few pulls on the bottle, but he was fine. Clear-headed. Ready and eager to do the right thing, though his gut was swarming with anxiety, and that rescue mission fantasy was beginning to feel a bit presumptuous. Hell, he didn't know a thing about his son Johnny.

It was his luck to arrive just as an event of some kind was breaking up. He could barely make out the Lodge through dust rolling off departing vehicles. He steered off the road and parked under a tree. He did not want to be recognized, nor could he suffer the mortification of being recognized and ignored. Better just to sit tight until they were gone.

When only a handful of couples were left lingering over good-bys he steered back to the road and slowly continued. A few heads turned his way but he hardly noticed. The landmark he was looking for was the three old brick barracks, but they had vanished as though swallowed up by the deep, dark gash in the grassy field where they used to stand. And where the hell did that big green tumor mounted on a pedestal come from? What was going on here? This was sacred ground. Old Camp Palmer was supposed to be eternal. It was not supposed to change. He wanted to hear rifle fire echo off Target Bluff and smell sunbaked canvas and the smoke of cook fires.

He had the road to himself and was soon headed uphill, away from the grassy basin. Thank God the Lodge still stood, forlorn and abandoned as it appeared. What an intimidating presence it had seemed back in his time. Through all those summer camps of the late thirties he'd kept his distance. The surrounding grounds had been the domain of starched, spit-shined, wide-brimmed Authority, where plans for low-life trainees like him were drawn up and judgement was passed. Get too close and lightning would strike. When you came to you'd be filling sandbags or up to your ankles in horse shit. Today the parking area in front of the porch was vacant, and he dared to guide his car into the commanding general's old slot.

He went up the steps to the porch and crossed to the door, which stood partway open. He hesitated at the threshold. His hand went to his shirt pocket. He was tempted to light up and take a break right there on the porch. Maybe out of curiosity young Spenser would approach him. He'd come such a long way. Let the boy make the final move to bring them together. But no, he was not going to piss around anymore. Full speed ahead, damn it.

He crossed the threshold. A welcoming aroma drifted over him, a stink of yesteryear's excesses. He breathed deeply of it. The floor and log walls were stripped bare. There was nothing to see.

The next room where the reunion banquets had been held was bigger and darker and smelled different – smoky and damp, but it was as barren as the first one. If this was a museum, his ass was the *Mona Lisa*.

The door to the kitchen was closed. Unlike the brown stained walls and ceiling rafters, it wore a thick coat of pale government green, although like everything else around here it was nicked up from long service. Even the frosted glass pane had been painted green. Hagan tapped on it lightly, then knocked on the wooden frame. No response. He shied away from speaking up and instead approached the last room.

Like the others it was stripped bare, but unlike them

there was an attached bathroom. The door was open and he heard water filling the toilet tank. Someone had recently flushed. In an otherwise abandoned building, who else would that be except the man in charge?

Well, here goes, he thought. He closed his eyes and took comfort thinking of his daughters, two terrific young women who knew him well and loved him even so. Whatever happened next would not change that. "Some museum you got here, Johnny, me boy! Bare walls and a great gloomy emptiness! ..."

There, he'd made his presence known to one and all. It was the kid's turn. Show yourself! Tell me what's going on.

His gaze shifted back to the green door. What to do? He wandered back to it. This time he didn't yell. He kept his voice low and calm.

"I don't know what your mother told you, Johnny, but I'm not so evil that you have to hide from me. Your Bold Eagle museum – wherever the hell it is – is my story too, you know. Did your mother tell you that I was one of the Drumlin boys that went off to war with the Bold Eagle? Now here I am, and there's no story, nothing but a hollowed-out old building, and no one around to explain."

The door was a flimsy thing. One good lunge and it would fly open. But as a different sort of barrier it was effective. What kind of guy would refuse to speak to his own father? What kind of guy would *hide* from his father? He started to pace, imagining what should have filled these empty walls: Aussie newspaper headlines screaming WAR!, photos of beaches as wide open and defenseless as drunken hookers, GIs marching down gangplanks onto

Australian soil, tent cities going up, soldiers on rifle and tommy gun ranges and trudging with full packs on route marches and finally rigged up in battle gear and mounting stairways into C-47s destined to carry them over sea and mountains into a long nightmare. And that was just the beginning. But the big room was dark and empty and smelled of mold. What a let-down. What a repudiation. From beginning to end the whole fucking trip.

Was this enough, he wondered? Had he done his duty? Rarely had visions of the long flight home, all that tedium and butt ache, held such a melancholy attraction for him. He was an old man who had made an honest effort to redress, in whatever shabby, half-assed way he could, a terrible wrong committed ages ago. Could he finally check this obligation off his list? Was he free to go home?

One last try. Back at the green door he said, "John, I've been the worst kind of dad to you – absent and out of touch. But I want you to know that you've been on my mind forever. Also that you have two delightful sisters, that you are an uncle to wonderful little girls, and that they would all be thrilled to make your acquaintance. And I can assure you as an expert in the matter that Melbourne, Australia, would be a most wonderful place to start life over. I'm tired of drinking alone. Let's spend some time together. You'd love Australia. Lovely people, lovely family who would make you very, very welcome."

Nothing. Not a sob, not a snicker. He paced again, back to the first room with its beery stink. The front door was open. Clouds had moved over the grassy basin. He could feel their chill. He had arrived at Old Camp on a late summer afternoon, but it was an autumn sky he looked out on now, and the chill was an autumn chill.

He marched back to the door and kicked it. "Hey Johnny, you got responsibilities here, right? A precious relic like this place needs protection from certain visitors, right? Like, say, some idiot with a cigarette. But damn it, I am weary and I need a smoke. When a guy gets old and weary and *pissed off* he can get mighty careless."

Nothing.

Hagan plucked a cigarette from his pocket, lit up, and got down on his knees. It wasn't easy. He sucked deeply on the cigarette, pressed his face to the floor and exhaled under the door. "Not smoking you out, am I?"

Nothing.

Back on his feet he wobbled for a moment, light-headed. Then he kicked the door again. "Come on, for Christ's sake. We're two grown men. Shake it off. I've had a very shitty couple of days, John. I plan to be on an airplane back to a friendlier world damn soon."

From the other side of the door came a sound like a sizzling jet of air. Stunned, he tried to unscramble it: a woman's voice, a desperate, clinging whisper: "Johnny!"

He couldn't believe it. He sagged, suddenly feeble and tremoring as though he might faint dead away, but his feet were still under him, and a great hot sense of wickedness was boiling up from within. *Her!* What was she doing here? Good Christ, was she still smothering the poor sap? The meddling bitch.

"I know what you're afraid of, Johnny, and it's not me," he said. "You're afraid of breaking free. Have you ever had a *really* good time? Ever set off on an adventure thinking, 'Let's see how this turns out'? Maybe you wake up in bed with a woman you don't recognize. Maybe you wake up in jail. Maybe you call the boss and tell him to fuck off. Anything like that ever happen to you?" He hesitated. "No, I don't think so, not with that woman hovering over you. What got drilled into you is that it's a scary world out there. That it's better to die of thirst than drink something that might be dangerous. That's what you grew up with, isn't it, Johnny? Hold your nose and tiptoe through the dark. And that's why you'll never feel like a complete man until you start life over far from her shadow. Melbourne worked for me. It could do the same for you."

Seconds went by. Still not a sound. "Well you know what they say – no guts, no glory. Last call, buddy." He dropped the cigarette and ground it into the floor. A shaky calm settled over him. What a fool he had been to expect anything different from these people – or from his own vile self. "The clock is ticking, and I've got a life to get back to." The stewardess would bring him vodka miniatures, as many as he could beg, then with any luck salad, steak, and a decent wine, and he would sleep, sleep, sleep across the whole damn ocean.

"Well then, shame on us both!"

* * *

She clung to his wrist as though it was her lifeline. They stared at each other. Her mouth moved silently: DON'T!... DON'T! She put a finger to her lips, but her strength was ebbing. Her face melted from anger to despair. Such vulnerability. It was an expression out of their distant past, and it paralyzed him now as it had back then. He tried to yank his arm free. After all, the man was talking to him, not her. He had a right. She couldn't deny him.

"Johnny!" she whispered.

She wouldn't let go, so he pried her fingers one by one and shook himself free, but free to do what?

All it would take was a twist of the lock, a twist of the knob.

His mother's face was buried in her hands. She was holding her breath.

He clasped the medallion in his pocket, squeezed his eyes shut. He clung to his talisman and waited. No, he wouldn't touch the doorknob, wouldn't say a word. Of course not, because he had already made up his mind. The only man he wanted in his life now was the one represented by the brass image clutched in his hot little hand.

"Last call, buddy. The clock is ticking..."

He listened to his thumping heart.

"Then shame on us both."

Footsteps again, fading.

They heard the car start. Spenser went back to the window, peering carefully, as though he was the guilty party.

"Is he gone?" she said.

"He's leaving."

"Is he going *away*?"

"Of course he's going away. What else could he do?"

"Where is he now?"

"He's already down to the road, heading out."

"Keep watching. I want to be sure. He can be very sneaky."

"Oh for Christ's sake, Mom."

"You don't know that man."

"You don't say. I wonder why."

"John!"

He was pissed off and he had a right to be, but just then, as though to rebuke him, the car pulled onto the grass. "Shit," he muttered.

"What?"

"He stopped."

"And...? What is he doing?"

"Getting out. He popped the trunk."

"I'm not surprised. There's probably a body in there."

"He's taking something out."

"What?"

"A box of some sort. He's coming around the passenger side. He put it on the seat."

"Are you sure it's not a bottle?"

"He's going back to the driver's side." Spenser paused a moment, then turned away from the window. "He's gone." He took a deep breath. "What have we done?"

He had just started guiding his mother's chair down the driveway when he noticed a woman below, standing beside his truck. Everyone else had cleared out, everyone but Sergeant High and Private Low. She had a scarf tied around her head and was shading her eyes. At first he couldn't place her, but then it was obvious. Louise, of course. Months ago she'd been his self-appointed greeter, passing on to him the key to the Lodge, and now, still loyal to the veterans who had not been loyal to her, she waited for him to give it back. "Thank goodness," she said as they came near. "I was afraid I'd miss you."

After belting his mother in and starting the truck he checked the rear-view mirror. Sure enough, Louise was trudging uphill to the Lodge. The building was empty and would soon be demolished, but as long as it stood it was still sacred. She had made a commitment to her brother and his dead buddies. She would make sure it was locked.

* * *

They were back on the interstate, heading south. "You okay?" he asked.

She was slow to respond. "Did you know?" she said.

She had thrust her head back to avoid the late sun. Her expressionless face gazed straight ahead but, he suspected, saw nothing. "About him? Of course I didn't know. How could I?"

Another long pause. "Lots of ways. You two could have been in touch."

It took him a moment to grasp what she was getting at. "Betrayed again, is that what you're saying? First your husband, now your son. The story of your life. Oh no you don't, Mom." Take it easy, he thought. Keep calm and carry on. "You know that didn't happen. I've done nothing to feel guilty about."

"But he was right, wasn't he? About me. About how a bitter woman might suffocate her son."

He thought about it, his eyes on the road. "I'm doing fine, Mom. No complaints. It wasn't easy for you, I know."

That was all they had to say for now. The sun was sinking behind the western hills, draining color from the fields. Out of the sky came the sound of gossiping geese, also heading south. Spenser had intended to stop for an early supper somewhere old-fashioned like a steak house or supper club. He'd have cut her steak into tiny pieces and mashed sour cream into her baked potato, and they would have taken their time. They would have found something to talk about. She had brought her four o'clock meds. There would have been no rush.

But all that was out of the question now. She needed to be alone. There was so much to sort out. A rare day with her son had blown up in her face. She was pondering the unthinkable – that he'd nearly gone over to the other side. He was certain of that. It was poison and she was tempted to drink it. Maybe she imagined that if she hadn't been there, what a wild, wicked time John and his father would have had together, partly at her expense. Or was she blaming herself? Something was boiling over behind those eyes, and it would take time for her to fret over it and bring it under control.

Spenser wasn't upset anymore. He knew he was home free. Nothing could shake him from the path he'd settled into already, not even after what they'd just been through. He liked his life in the nearly vacant BOQ, liked his little office in the old barracks. He felt a small-town kinship with the girls in the commissary and the PX and the mailroom woman so worried about his weight that she was forever foisting homemade sweets on him. The pressure was off. He already knew how the next three years would pass, the rest of the Bold Eagle's war in the Pacific to organize, though as far as he was concerned everything after Ponga was an afterthought. Ponga would forever be the centerpiece. It was what set the Bold Eagle apart. So, sure, he'd have plenty of collecting and cataloguing to do in the off chance that the museum was ever brought back to life. But what he looked forward to most of all was getting back to his grandfather's books with their warnings of crises ahead; enemies on the march! Freedom in peril! Wake up, America! Wake up! To arms! To arms! He would sink back into the world war state of mind, local men in danger far from home, a fear of telegrams, days filled with humdrum routine but the mind always elsewhere, brooding. This was that war that made him, and immersed back into that war was where he belonged.

Eventually he would be drawn back to the house on the hill with all those empty rooms, but by then he would be deep into a project of his own. It would carry him through those solitary afternoons when the lives he might have lived came back to taunt him and when that commanding figure returned to loom over his shoulder and whisper, "Still stuck on the Disney version, I see." But if the museum was destined to languish in storage, he would carry on, telling the story as he was convinced it should be told. A good man had been written out of history by lesser men. Spenser knew research. He could put sentences together. He'd already spent much of his life writing reports for other people. Now, with luck, he could spend the rest of his life lost in a project that really mattered.

So he wasn't mad. He was grateful that his mother felt safe and secure in Park Manor. He was relieved that he would soon be back in his new apartment at Camp Palmer. He was glad the summer soldiers were gone until next year and that the staff of year 'rounders was settling in for another season of isolation from the world.

Before they got home he'd find something to say. He just wanted her to be at peace with herself even if, like him, that meant living in the past.

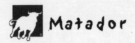Matador